Indian River County Main Library
1600 21st Street
Vero Beach, FL 32960

DEEP FREEZE

TRAITORS
DIE

D.S. WEISSMAN

EPIC
Press

Traitors Die
Deep Freeze: Book #5

Written by D.S. Weissman

Copyright © 2017 by Abdo Consulting Group, Inc.

Published by EPIC Press™
PO Box 398166
Minneapolis, MN 55439

Printed in the United States of America.

Cover design by Dorothy Toth
Images for cover art obtained from iStockPhoto.com
Edited by Melanie Austin

LIBRARY OF CONGRESS CATALOGING-IN-PUBLICATION DATA

Names: Weissman, D.S., author.
Title: Traitors die / by D.S. Weissman.
Description: Minneapolis, MN : EPIC Press, [2017] | Series: Deep freeze ; book #5
Summary: The outliers have disappeared into the mountains. Abe has failed the settlement in
 his inability to capture James, but no one can take Abe's place as chief. The war between
 the outliers and the settlement must end, but no one is ready to do what needs to be done,
 except Abe.
Identifiers: LCCN 2015959395 | ISBN 9781680760194 (lib. bdg.) |
 ISBN 9781680762853 (ebook)
Subjects: LCSH: Adventure and adventurers—Fiction. | Interpersonal relationships—Fiction. |
 Survival—Fiction. | Human behavior—Fiction. | Young adult fiction.
Classification: DDC [Fic]—dc23
LC record available at http://lccn.loc.gov/2015959395

EPICPRESS.COM

To my teachers who encouraged me to write more, but also told me never to show my writing to them because my spelling was terrible

CALL TO THE WILD

CHARLOTTE

THE DOGS BARKED IN THE ASHEN HAZE OF THE SHIFTING morning, before the light had a chance to inch into the cave that had become Charlotte's home. The dogs weren't puppies any more, at least in the way they looked—fully formed, shaggy, dirty, strong, lean. The dogs had become a part of the outliers, once nestled in Autry's arms that first night in the cold, dark cave. Now the dogs nudged Charlotte's arm trying to wake her, to get her up and out into the forest to hunt. The dogs made the hunt easier, even though no one had eaten a decent meal for six months. If hunting and surviving were hard before, they now felt impossible. Charlotte hadn't had a full bath since they left the ship.

When the need for cleanliness overcame her, she retreated into the cave, close to the dim light of a seemingly endlessly dwindling fire. It was the closest she had gotten to a bath. The fire burned hot enough to keep part of her warm. She undressed herself one limb at a time to keep the stale cold from her exposed body. She rubbed a coarse rag up and down her skin. She scrubbed her arm, leg, groin, armpit, neck, face, feet—especially her feet, an area that oscillated between sweat-soaked and frozen— her other arm and other leg. She had become adept at the slow and controlled movements, almost graceful. Each stride took away a layer of hard dirt. The times she bathed left her feeling human; the longer she went without clean skin, the longer she forgot about the putrid body odor she once tried to hide. The less she cared about cleanliness, the less she worried about feeling human at all, the less she bothered being human.

"Okay," Charlotte said. "I'm up." She mumbled into James's ear. He didn't stir. Her stuffed walrus, Franklin, lay in the small crevice of her arms, snuggled close to her chest. His whiskers bristled against her chin when she moved. The dogs growled and pressed their butts into the air. Charlotte could feel her bloodshot eyes, in need of rest, but refused a night away from anxiety.

She had never before felt the stabbing, unquenchable pain of hunger. Over the past months, lethargy had reared its ugly head. Everyone was too tired—which meant too weak—to go out hunting every day, even if it would solve the issue. More trips meant more food. She was tired too; she didn't want the outliers to see it. The less everyone else hunted the weaker they became and the stronger she needed to become.

Hunger ran up her throat and tried to swallow her tongue at times. It absorbed whatever fat she had left on her body, around her ribs, sinking her cheeks. Sometimes the worst thing that could happen was for her, James, Phil, or Cheryl to find food. She and James had agreed to let the other kids eat before them. Somewhere along the line she preferred to go hungry rather than to wait for food to cook, rather than wait in line watching the food, smelling the food. The inability to touch the food hurt more than the hunger. A leader had to make sacrifices, she realized, but it didn't mean she liked it.

Charlotte grabbed the bow and arrow and followed the two pups Autry had named Lee and Gray out of the cave. The light moved slowly over the trees. When they came into the canopy, her eyes adjusted to the dark, frosty haze. The dogs had been in competition on the island, fighting for the top of the food chain. Charlotte couldn't walk through the forest without thinking of the night the people and the dogs finally clashed. They had danced around each other long enough. The dogs were the sole reason more people hadn't been hurt, even if Gray and Lee were among the last of the remaining feral creatures on the island.

Gray had more white fur than gray, if he had any gray at all, while Lee was draped in gray, like the underwhelming stretch of clouds that sat over the island during the day. Charlotte followed them through the trees while they sniffed and huffed, winding around one another and venturing deeper under the canopy in search of any food they could find.

The dogs led her to familiar ground, where she looked at the crusted trees, the snow-riddled forest floor, and broken branches. She remembered running through the forest with a sack filled with contraband, cans that clanked against one another in the darkness. Her heart pounded, hoping no one heard the cans or her heartbeat on those stolen nights. If Charlotte could, she would skulk back to the settlement in the hopes that someone would sneak her a crumb. They didn't need to hunt and had enough resources to last years if they needed. Or their stocks could be left to rot, if Abe wanted.

Charlotte imagined what the settlement made

for breakfast. The simple tastes of hot oatmeal with a side of eggs made her mouth water. The closest thing they had to eggs now came in powdered form and tasted better than any eggs she remembered. She couldn't remember the flavor of certain foods because she hadn't tasted them in so long. The days of her lurking in the space around the settlement were long over. She shouldn't have wandered this close now. She herded the dogs away from the forest's edge, worried that someone would spot her sifting through the underbrush.

She could hear the faint sizzle of deer bacon. Pork bacon didn't exist; the last time she heard deer bacon sizzle on a skillet was before James fought Geoff in the Icedome. Her stomach didn't even growl at the thought of food. More than her mind, it understood that cravings and memories didn't satisfy hunger.

Gray and Lee nudged Charlotte's leg and ran into the distance. That meant deer, and deer meant food. She raced after them as fast as she could. They were more nimble, more energetic. They didn't have the emaciated, dry, crusted spots Charlotte saw on the majority of the outliers. Some of them started to talk openly about returning to the settlement. But they wouldn't—they couldn't. Going back was suicide. It didn't satisfy their hunger, but it gave them a moment to look forward to.

"I don't think I can do it," James had told Charlotte.

"You're the best chance anyone here has," she said.

"Why can't anyone else come up with a plan? I'm tired. I'm just tired." Her fingers stuck to his thick, oily hair.

"We all are," she said.

"Why can't someone else do it?" he asked. "Why do I always have to? The last plan I came up with ended with me killing . . . " His voice trailed off. Charlotte noticed James hadn't said Geoff's name since the day in the Icedome, the day James stabbed Geoff in the heart. She wouldn't make him say it.

"You'll think of something," she said. "You always have. They'll wait for you to come up with something."

"I'm worried they'll wait too long."

Now, in the distance, a deer stood on its hind legs and pressed its forelegs against the tree. It nibbled cold leaves from the lowest branches. The deer was smaller than Charlotte hoped, somewhere between calf and adolescent. Gray and Lee stood by Charlotte and ducked behind the brush. They stayed quiet like Charlotte, lying low by her side. She pulled the bow from around her shoulder. The deer had finished all the edible leaves on the lower branches. It popped down. *Still hungry*, she thought. *Everything on the island must be hungry.* The deer dug its hooves into the snow, like a dog burying a bone. It pressed and pushed until the dirt and snow opened up. The deer knocked at the plant roots, finding life deeper in the soil, sustained away from the freeze. *Why hadn't I thought of that?* They could have had roots this entire time. She could leave the deer alone, opt for the roots, and start digging. The deer continued to graze. Its pallid fur shook a little as it ate. Charlotte's mouth watered as much from the root as from the deer. She didn't want to wait, but the wrong plant could end in disaster.

She tucked an arrow into the bow, pulled the string, and when she felt herself breathe slow and controlled with the deer, she let the string loose, hitting the small animal in its torso. When Charlotte stood up, Gray and Lee ran to the staggering animal. The deer didn't run. The scent of warm metal rose from the animal's wound. The blood spilled onto the ground. Sometimes she wondered if the snow melted or the blood froze. The drops created a smiley face, and more drops smeared across the snow adding whiskers to the smiles.

The face looked like Franklin, her stuffed walrus, down to the beady, piercing eyes. It was surprising he had lasted this long, not thrown into a fire for a sad sense of immediate warmth. Franklin persisted, the same way the outliers did. That was the real reason she held onto him.

The most important people in Charlotte's life had passed Franklin to her—first her parents, then James when he had found Franklin sitting in an abandoned cupboard when their city burned around them. Charlotte's father had given Franklin to her when she was young enough to love stuffed animals for their cuteness, their comfort, but old enough to be embarrassed by them and the rest of her stuffed animal collection.

"He made me think of you," her dad had said. He walked through the door after a weeklong business trip to Norway. Charlotte held the walrus close, and his whiskers brushed against her shoulder, back in a time when she could show skin, and in a city where cold rarely existed and a tank top didn't mean imminent overexposure.

"I love him," she said. She didn't tell her father that days earlier her friend Shannon came over, took one look at Charlotte's bed, and scoffed.

"It's full of stuffed animals," Shannon had said.

"I don't know why," Charlotte lied. "Must have been my mom. She still thinks I'm a kid." She tried to imitate the sound Shannon had made, emphasized by her hand on her hip. The shame in Charlotte's stomach twisted like rancid milk. She and Shannon never entered her room and painted their nails in the living room with MTV loud in the background. Charlotte had never painted her nails before. She borrowed some of her mom's polish, a scarlet color she had never seen her mom wear.

"We'll look so fab," Shannon said, imitating one of the girls they heard on TV.

They sat and stroked the tiny brush over their toes. It tickled at first. The fumes made Charlotte dizzy. Halfway through Charlotte stood up to use the bathroom.

"Careful not to smear it," Shannon said.

Charlotte waddled like a penguin to the bathroom, her toes pointed up, the paint blobbed over her toenails. She half expected the paint to ooze onto her skin and the carpet. She wanted to flap her arms as she walked but suppressed the impulse. *I'm not a child anymore*, she thought. *I'm using nail polish now.* But the urge to joke, laugh, quack, and snuggle her bed full of stuffed animals hadn't subsided. Wasn't that supposed to leave when she became a woman? Maybe she had to push it out by using makeup, by acting like an adult. It started with the nail polish.

After Shannon left, Charlotte grabbed a trash bag from the kitchen and stuffed it with her entire collection. Biggles, the bear she had gotten when her parents went camping in Yosemite. Martin, the moose her dad had bought her in Canada. Johan, the yeti her parents gave her after a trip to Switzerland. Charlotte soon realized each animal reminded her of a trip her parents had taken; one she hadn't gone on. The animals started to look like penance, bought by her parents because of their guilt, given to Charlotte to ease their shame. She packed the trash bag and hauled it out the door to the garbage cans, a perverse Santa carrying shameful toys in a sack filled with what people brought back when they left Charlotte behind.

That night her mom noticed the empty space on Charlotte's bed.

"Where are all your stuffed animals?" she asked.

"I'm almost twelve now, Mom."

"So?" she said. "I'm older than twelve and I love stuffed animals."

"You're a mom."

"Oh," she said. "So it's okay for me but you're too cool for them now?"

The warmth of an angry blush flashed across Charlotte's face.

"That's not what I meant," she snapped.

"Tell me what you meant," her mom said. "You loved those animals."

If you had taken me with you I wouldn't have

needed those animals, Charlotte thought. She stormed off to her room. The lack of animal presence stuffed the bed with awkward space. When Charlotte's dad came home two days later the walrus reminded her too much of the friends she had given up, the games she had played, the times they all acted as a mattress when she jumped off her bed and they caught her, and the anger of where they came from, the places she hadn't gone. She hugged the walrus, squeezed her dad—as her mom watched from the kitchen—and Charlotte ran up the stairs to her room. The walrus didn't fit on her bed now—not physically speaking, but emotionally. Its beady eyes never stopped staring. They asked her about other animals to sit with, about others to play with so she wouldn't be so lonely. Its eyes always stayed open, nudging her, asking her, judging her, "Why did you do it?" the eyes asked. "They were your friends too."

Charlotte took the walrus and shoved it in her closet, deep down with the board games she no

longer played, hidden under the Halloween costumes she couldn't fit in. The scarlet nails applauded
her. She told them to shut up.

She found the walrus almost three years later
when a woman in a pantsuit with a waxy face met
Charlotte in her room. Charlotte's parents had been
in a car crash. She had spent time at the hospital,
then at a friend's, then ten minutes at her house
rubbing her fingers against the walls, touching the
tangible difference of each room, the house filled
with the faint scent of noxious fumes from the
memory of her painted toes, absent of the musty
stuffed animals.

"We have to be quick," Pamela said.

Charlotte looked through her closet for clothes.
She stumbled over the old Halloween costumes,
a crappy, torn Tinker Bell dress, and found the
walrus. She stared at his silent, beady eyes. The
walrus said nothing now.

"He looks nice," Pamela said, framed by the
doorway, the way her mother used to stand, except

this woman was nothing like her mother. Charlotte could smell Pamela, a combination of sandalwood and antibacterial cream. Charlotte didn't want Pamela in her room, taking over the familiar scent, the comfortable scent. "What's his name?"

"Franklin," Charlotte said.

"That's a great name."

It was my father's name, Charlotte thought. "Thanks," she said.

"We need to get going," Pamela said. Her scent had already crept into the room, smothering whatever connection Charlotte had left with the new, old house.

"Okay," Charlotte said. She didn't take much with her but refused to leave Franklin behind.

In the cold of the extending forest, Charlotte stood over her kill. The deer blinked. She needed to take the deer back to the cave. It wouldn't feed everyone.

Blood continued to drip and overtook the walrus face in the snow. She needed to find another deer, even one of the same size, to help them all eat, maybe for more than one day, or two, or even five. If the deer stayed unguarded it wouldn't be here when Charlotte returned, she was sure. The sooner she got it back to the cave the faster everyone could eat—the faster she could eat. But the deer would slow her down in another hunt.

Gray and Lee sat by Charlotte's feet. They licked their snouts. Charlotte's stomach gurgled. What if she didn't take the deer back to the cave at all? It couldn't feed everyone anyway. Then they would have to choose who would get their fill of the deer and who would go hungry. More likely they would make a stew, a watered-down amalgamation of stringy meat and snow, and everyone would get enough to satisfy themselves for an hour, leaving everyone hungry, angry, sad, malnourished. If she came back to camp without a kill, but also without hunger she would be able to focus, help them all survive, not rely on James as a single hope, and not be pulled away every minute by thoughts of herself back in the settlement eating powdered eggs whisked into a scramble.

The deer's empty eyes stared up at Charlotte. The dogs' hungry eyes stared at the deer. If Charlotte could look at herself she would see her dull yellow skin and oddly bright eyes bulging out of her head. The deer's blood spilled out. Charlotte dropped to her knees and pulled the arrow from the body. Charlotte needed to share. She could smell the heavy iron in the blood. The body was still warm. The dogs stayed seated. Charlotte pressed her hands to the deer's flesh, dipped her lips to the open wound, and started to drink. It was wrong, she knew, the types of disease she could contract, but when the thick sanguine touched her lips and spilled down her throat she never wanted to stop drinking. It filled her mouth. She sucked against the deer fur. She pressed her lips harder against the skin. Her stomach started to fill, hot and heavy. She pushed herself away, scrambling backwards to the ground. The world spun around her, open to the firm steel sky. Gray and Lee lapped up the crimson from her cheeks. And chin. Their tongues were warm. The daylight was barely better than the night.

The deer was dead. She needed to take it back to the cave. She looked into the sky and screamed so hard it shook and burned her throat. She let it tumble into the air and shake the leaves. She screamed again. The dogs started to howl. They all screamed together.

A DIFFERENT KIND OF HUNGER

ABE

IN THE MORNING ABE LOOKED OUT OVER THE LANDSCAPE, BLIStering light reflecting off the snow. He blinked and saw spots. The colors ran around his peripheral vision as he followed the dots along the tree line into nowhere. The sky's gunmetal color penetrated the snow and blinded anyone who looked directly at the bleached landscape.

Within the forceful limits of the light and the continued frozen leaves, Abe couldn't help but turn over the memory of that night in the forest. He had stood close enough to James to see his eyes alight with fear. Abe swore in the cold of the night, under the canopy where the stars were absent, in the clouds of bursting breaths, that he could smell James's rancidity singeing the lower branches of the forest. It smelled like gasoline. He remembered the scent of gasoline from when he had soaked some of the cruise ship in petrol so that the halls and the quarters would burn long after he left. For a while, the smell followed him around, stained in his clothes, on his skin, beneath his fingernails. He had stopped eating with his hands out of fear he would inadvertently taint his food. As the days, weeks, and even months passed, the smell didn't fade, not from his clothes, not from his skin. No matter how much he scrubbed he couldn't escape it. At one point Elise had asked him what was wrong.

"Nothing," he said as he hid his fingers behind his back.

"What's wrong with your fingers?" she asked.

"Nothing," he said again, but when he showed her his nails they were less than nubs. He had torn the top layer of skin away. It shriveled and bled in the heat of their bedroom. She had stopped the smell from overpowering him, but the awful odor of life overwhelmed him once Elise left. Abe had trouble with all the smells he had never noticed before. Even the frozen trees had a particular sourness that burned his nostrils. Wherever he went, instead of gasoline, he smelled shit, or piss, or vomit, or stale fish heads. As he walked from his room to the dining hall in the over-lit gray day, he wished for a storm to wash away all the smells but the ones he missed: the fruity aroma of Elise, the salty ocean, asphalt in the rain, and fresh bacon grease. Those were all out of reach; he couldn't capture them ever again, and the lingering smell of rotten meat sprung from his swollen black finger.

Abe didn't enter the dining hall; instead he walked into the kitchen. It had been months since the incident in the woods and he still felt like a failure. The settlement had watched as the outliers got away. The wild dogs that attacked in the night hurt people who shouldn't have been there in the first place. Abe had the responsibility to protect the settlement and all those in it, but he hadn't. The rules were clear: if anyone in charge endangers those they were charged with protecting, they would incur punishment and have to resign. It was up to the discretion of the committee. But Abe knew what he deserved. He should feel frozen air against his bare skin, wrapping around him like ice picks tapping at the outer layer of his body until it seeped into his orifices and stabbed at his insides too, slush coating his tongue and freezing the muscle to his teeth. Then they'd thaw him out and do it again so he could understand how disappointment felt.

"Cold?" Shia asked.

"What?" Abe asked. Abe wondered if Shia could read his thoughts. Every night since the forest Abe debated stepping out into the center square and stripping his clothes away. No one else accused him of breaking the rules but he knew what he had done. Shia had meant hello, in the way that everyone greeted one another—that was all.

"Morning," Shia said. "You okay?"

Powdered eggs smelled similar to old oatmeal, filled with bits of mold. Extra deer meat sizzled in the pan. It was about to turn. Abe wouldn't allow the settlement to waste anything: meat, clothing, it didn't matter. Whatever you took you needed to account for. Meat about to turn could still feed people. Eat the old meat before you eat the new meat. Tear the old clothes to patch up the new clothes. Use already cut wood to patch up the buildings. Abe could smell the slime that covered the larger cuts of meat Shia slid into the pans. Grease sizzled and splattered off the griddle.

"Yeah," Abe said. He took a plate and filled it with the eggs and meat that had already been cooked. He put the plate on a large table as the rest of the kids in the kitchen avoided him like a stream around a boulder. There were no seats in the kitchen. Used bowls, splattered batter, and cutlery covered the long prep table; every fork, knife, spoon, plate, bowl, and glass was accounted for. Abe took a fork and cut the deer meat, sliding its edge from front to back until the slice separated from the slab. He used his middle finger for leverage against the metal, avoiding his index finger. The black tip ached, the dead muscle never revived. Instead the edges turned green and started to spread toward his knuckle. The stench and the fact he couldn't escape it infuriated him.

The deer meat was chewy and dry. The food hadn't been the same since Tic-Tac left. He hadn't cooked often but he at least knew how to make the meat tender and flavorful. Months had passed since Abe had eaten a satisfying meal. The stocks were full but dwindling. The greenhouse wasn't producing as much as he had hoped, not since Charlotte and Autry left. Soon the plants would die like the world around them. People had followed James and then the settlement came crashing down in their absence. If something didn't change soon, everyone else would know it too.

"The deer could use salt," Abe said. He stared

at the mixture of tasteless rubbery meat and muddy eggs.

"We're rationing," Shia said.

"It could still use salt."

"Then let us go get some."

Abe looked up. Shia kept his eyes on the large skillet containing at least four pieces of meat that sizzled and popped.

Other kids poured out the doors to the dining hall with plates and cutlery in hand. Abe wasn't sure if it was time to set the tables or if they wanted to escape the simmering tension between Abe and Shia.

"What happened to the salt from last week's rations?" Abe asked.

"We used it," Shia said. He stabbed the meat with a fork and pushed the pieces around smoldering fat. "We're supposed to get new rations every week, Abe." Shia looked up, straight at Abe. "Of course we don't have any salt. I told the rest of them it was because we have to pick and choose what we use it for now."

"That's right," Abe said. "We do."

Shia let go of the skillet and the fork dropped into the grease with the meat.

"You have to be kidding," Shia said. "We have plenty of salt. And vegetables. And tomatoes. We don't need to ration like this."

"If you don't like it . . . " Abe said. Shia had grown since they reached the island, since the forest. He had palled around with Tic-Tac so often Abe hadn't noticed Shia change, even though he was on the committee. He had shaggy hair and an insecure smile. When he led them all to the liquor store in San Diego, he couldn't even tell Abe what side was up. Now he had the balls to tell Abe how they should ration the stocks. "The door hasn't moved."

"If you want salt, make it your damn self," Shia said. He took off his apron and threw it onto the table that now sat empty of everything but leftover batter and Abe's food. He made his way to the dining hall.

"You think this is what I want?" Abe asked.

Shia stopped short of the door. "No one knows what the hell you want." He opened the door and stepped into the loud calls of the hungry.

Abe wanted to protect the settlement at all costs, from whatever threats there were, even the ones from within. No one else could lead the settlement like he could. He sunk his teeth into the rubbery meat without cutting it.

The familiar howls of wild dogs broke through the kitchen. Abe remembered being hog-tied in the cruise ship, James holding a knife to his nuts and giving up before Abe even gave in. No one knew what it took to lead. It wasn't a matter of what you did, but what you could do—what you would do. Abe would do anything that needed to be done.

SICKENING
CABIN FEVER

JAMES

QUIET ENCOMPASSED THE CAVE BEFORE THE MAJORITY OF the outliers stirred. James sat at the mouth of the cave and waited for Charlotte to return. He had felt tired the past weeks as food became scarce and his world shrunk to an open cave. The early air pressed against his cheeks. He didn't want to put his hood up. Somehow, in the warmth of his clothes, now that he didn't leave the cave, his hood felt claustrophobic and suffocating. His cough no longer burned but corroded. One day James sat outside the cave's mouth, with his hood on, for what felt like an hour. He coughed into the emptiness and spat whatever fluid he brought up. The colors fluctuated from defined chunky yellow to thinning red. Pigments swirled into disgusting tie-dye separated like oil and vinegar. The day slowly stole the color from his cheeks. He didn't need anyone to tell him life would become harder.

Dogs howled in the distance. It was a good sign, a way to know where Charlotte was in the woods, hollow of most life. Autry came and sat next to James.

"I'm hungry," she said rubbing her eyes.

"Me too," James said. "It's okay to say it."

"It doesn't help," Autry said.

"No. It doesn't."

Autry rested her head against James's shoulder. "Where's Charlotte?" Autry asked.

"Helping," James said.

Autry closed her eyes. James looked out over the sunken trees and waited for the branches or the trees to rustle, the earth to split open. Two dogs followed Autry around, Sand and Diego.

Charlotte had named them.

"Why Sand and not San?" James asked.

"Because I miss sand," Charlotte said. "Hot, powdery sand."

"What about Diego?"

"It just sounds pretty. We can all use a little more beauty in our lives."

"At least you can remember the sand," James said. Charlotte then nuzzled close to James. In the cave's dryness, absent of oceanic memories, James tried to recall the sea salt in the air and the grittiness of the sand stuck under his fingernails, the collection of these smells drifting from Charlotte's hair. He couldn't do it.

"We need to talk," a boy's voice came from behind him, slow and low. Diego and Sand perked up but lay back down when Autry didn't move.

James turned his head, not wanting to wake Autry. The outline of a stocky boy stood in miniscule light. His shoulders were broad, but like the rest of them, he had emaciated cheeks from months in the cave.

"Sit," James said.

"I'd rather stand," Zack said. Now that Zack had lost his gut he looked taller. He looked stronger too, any loose skin now clung tight to his muscles. His unshaven face looked thicker and more formed than most of the other boys.

"Then stand," James said. Autry didn't move. The dogs huffed. Zack stood next to James. He kept looking out over the forest.

"A few of us are thinking about leaving," Zack said.

"Where you going to go?" James asked. They had a better chance of surviving if they all stayed together. It meant they could defend one another, and more importantly, it meant they would share their catches, not have to fight more people for less food. James also wanted to make sure that anyone who left wouldn't return to the settlement, for their—and his—own good.

"We want out," Zack said. "We're cold and we're starving. It's time to go."

In San Diego, Zack had been quiet. Not frail, but not talkative. James remembered Zack's brother, Aaron, better. Aaron had been Zack's protector, and for the first year, Zack's voice. Zack would whisper into his brother's ear before saying anything to anyone. It was Aaron's protective nature that got him in trouble. Some hardcore kids were pushing around a girl Aaron didn't even know outside The Casbah, a concert venue. When he tried to step in, the girl ran, Aaron got stabbed, and Zack had to learn to speak for himself. *He finally learned*, James thought.

"Why do you get to leave when the rest of us don't?" James asked.

"Come with," Zack said. "But we can't stay here."

"You didn't answer my question," James said. "Where are you going to go?" Autry nestled her head against James's shoulder. The dogs perked up at her movement, then pressed their heads between their paws.

"We can't pretend . . . " Zack stammered. He leaned closer to James and whispered. "We can't pretend we can survive here, especially after Charlene . . . "

Zack's inflection sounded like he wanted to continue but he made no motion to talk. Charlene was a face James wouldn't forget. She hadn't been in Fornland for long before the endless winter fell. She hung out mostly with younger kids outside of James's radar. She was part hero, part involuntary lab rat. It came a few months after they all settled into the cave when the first real signs of hunger started to set in. Everyone complained about the pain in their stomachs. James had had a headache that pounded behind his eyes. Cheryl and Phil had gone on a hunt and seen a deer nibbling on blush-red berries that looked like plump ladybugs. They had brought back the deer and the berries.

"How'd they grow?" Charlotte had asked.

"Who cares?" Phil asked. "We can find them,

pick them, and live out here forever now!" His smile beamed. *The savior of them all*, it said.

Everyone wanted to be the hero, James remembered thinking. *No one wanted the sacrifice.*

"Where's the blood?" James asked. He had been watching the deer. There were no signs of an arrow wound, no signs of struggle.

"Well . . . " Cheryl said.

"Well, nothing," James said. "You brought back berries and a deer with no puncture wounds. Do the math. Those are poisonous. If they're not we shouldn't take the chance. Get them out of here before someone gets hungry enough to eat them."

"But—" Phil said.

"If we can't eat them, then why are we going to look at them?" James asked.

"Maybe we could boil them?" Cheryl asked.

"She's right," Charlotte said. "We could boil them. It may neutralize the toxins."

"Who's going to check?"

"I will," Charlotte said. Her eyes were hungry to

prove something, but James wasn't sure what. "I'll take just a small taste to make sure, after I boil them for a long while."

That night Charlotte boiled the berries. She counted twelve hundred seconds, took the berries out of the water and let them rest. She was going to put them back in the water for another three hundred seconds. James listened to the slow and methodical rhythm of Charlotte's voice when she counted downward. It almost lulled him to sleep. The room had been cool and quiet. The outliers huddled near the mouth of the cave. They had eaten deer and settled comfortably around Tic-Tac who tried to tell them stories about San Diego, as if it were a paradise. When Charlotte turned around she noticed two berries missing from the bundle.

"James," she said, "if the berries weren't poisonous it would mean someone had extra food; everyone else is hungry."

"We have to tell them," he said.

"Who took the berries?" Charlotte asked the

room. Her voice bounced off of the cold walls. They tried to account for guilty or missing faces. No one fessed up and they could do nothing. If Charlene had spoken up earlier, maybe they—maybe James— could have saved her. That night they heard the first throes of poison when Charlene wretched just beyond the cave's mouth. Cold sweat fell from her forehead, vomit crusted around her lips and her chin. She lost water, too weak to stand. By morning she was dead. No one else wanted any berries.

"I came in with Charlotte," Zack referenced the boardinghouse. "I would never do anything to compromise this place or you guys. Charlotte's the closest thing to a mom I've had since my mom slammed that coffee pot over that asshole's head."

"Sounded like he deserved it," James said.

"It was a diner, not a strip club," Zack said. "The point is she got fired and a twenty-year conviction." Zack and his brother got their young lives sentenced to Fornland. James knew the fierce loyalty the boardinghouse brought, but the cave had taught him the fragility of loyalty.

"Where are you going?" James asked again, emphasizing each word. Zack must want to go back to the settlement. James almost died too many times because of Abe. James couldn't let people return to that crazy asshole because life as an outlier was harder than they thought it would be. They all left the settlement for a reason. Abe would torture and kill anyone that returned to the settlement, and then he'd come for the rest of them.

"You can't go back," James said.

"I wasn't going to—"

"You can't go back."

Zack looked at the hard ground. His eyes started to water, but he never blinked and the tears never dropped.

"We're hungry," he said. "We can't keep going like this. We want to go."

"Because it'll be better there."

"At least there we can eat."

"I can't stop you from leaving here, but I will stop you from going back there."

"No you won't." He started to walk out of the cave. Soft footsteps echoed through the hole in the mountain in an attempt to follow.

"I won't let you," James said.

"I didn't realize we needed permission," Zack said.

"Now you do."

Autry rolled against James's shoulder. The dogs sat up. He had to stand between Zack and the entrance, the deserters and the settlement. If he didn't, no one would.

Zack stepped closer to James. His eyes burned and his face was thinner and hairier than James noticed in the dark. He cracked his knuckles and breathed heavily. James braced himself for a hard hit. But the hit never came.

Charlotte stood at the cave's entrance and sounded short of breath. Gray and Lee ran around James's legs before climbing over Autry. Diego and

Sand barked. Their tails wagged aggressively. Autry giggled and the dogs yipped. Zack stepped away. "Things look heated," Charlotte said.

"No," Zack said. "We wanted to—" James followed Zack's look. Charlotte was out of breath, but not just from the walk to the cave. She held onto a small deer and a large net woven out of leaves. He didn't know how she carried them up the hill but he didn't care. She was here, they had food, and no one needed to fight.

"Wanted to what?" Charlotte asked.

"Hunt," Zack said. "We wanted to help today but we didn't know where you were."

"Good," she said. "You can help by taking care of these." She dropped the carcass and net on the floor. "Gut them, save all you can, and let's make a stew."

"What's in the net?" Zack asked.

"You know all the fish we always thought were under the ice?" Charlotte asked.

James opened the net and a bundle of large salmon poured out. "But how'd you—"

"Saw them through a crack in the ice. The hard part was making the net."

"You hauled this by yourself?" James asked.

"Lee and Gray helped." She leaned in, kissed James on the nose, and whispered, "They took some off my back. Our little secret."

"You could have fallen," he said.

"But I didn't. Now there's enough food for everyone."

"You could—"

"I didn't." She looked at his eyes and he felt powerless. "I'm back." The words were soft. "We have food. That's what matters."

"A stew," James said to Zack. "It'll last longer." Zack nodded, took the deer and fish and walked back into the depths of the cave.

"Did you think I wouldn't come back?" Charlotte asked.

"Glad to see that deer on your shoulder," James said. "And you."

"Never been accused of that." She went to help prepare the food.

"They can handle it," James said.

"And I need to handle them," she said. Once the outliers ate they would come to their senses. Zack was right; they couldn't stay in the cave much longer. But if there was one thing James had learned since San Diego: you can never go back. Charlotte went to help prepare the stew. No one knew how to gut a fish, debone it, and tear away the scales and skin, at least not as far as James knew. They had learned about deer the hard way. At least Tic-Tac won't hurl this time.

In every attempt to survive, a person could eat an entire deer for themselves, worried about their next meal. If they wanted to survive, they needed to remember the group was stronger when fed. Zack had hit the wall of trying. The harsh hunger pains brought about the looming fear of death. *He might not have been too far gone for another meal to help,*

James thought. They could all survive together; they had lasted this long.

James coughed. It tore at the fabric of his insides. It left him gasping for air. He sat down ready to pass out or suffocate, but did neither.

INITIAL PURITY

ABE

ABE SAT ON THE FLOOR IN HIS ROOM WITH A KNIFE IN HIS hand. The blade was sharp. He dug its edge deep into the wood floor for the fourth time. He had powdered eggs in his teeth. The powder must not have dissolved completely. The grainy texture ran along his gums. He shoved the knife deeper into the wood. The hard surface peeled away.

Æ

Every time he carved one of the letters it made him feel less anxious, less tired. When he finished the connection of both letters he felt secure and whole. Once the letters stared back, the unbearable weight of emptiness crashed down on him, so he started carving again. He peeled away more of the wood and let the letters stare back at him, each one deeper than the last. If he could make the connections deep enough, pressing them into the floor, scorching them into the ground, part of him thought it could bring Elise back, or steal him back to a time when their initials together meant something tangible.

The door opened and Kelsey walked in. She sat on Abe's bed. Her knees were at his shoulders. He continued to strip the wood.

"You weren't at breakfast," she said. Her hair dripped over her face. She wore a coat that looked thicker than usual, heavy and hunter green. "I thought you might be hungry." She placed a plate down on his bed.

"Plates aren't supposed to leave the kitchen," he said. He carved another *A*.

"Neither are knives," she said. He stayed silent. "You have to eat."

"I did eat," he said. He started to carve another *E* but stopped. He looked back at Kelsey. She pushed the long red hair from her face. "There are no exceptions." Exceptions were what made the world turn to snow—what allowed Elise to carve her future into her wrists. Exceptions only made excuses, for the next person to pervert what had happened, turning an understandable situation into an untenable one. He held up the knife as an example of complacency. The small smile on Kelsey's face flatlined.

"I can take the plate back," she said.

"I'm sorry," Abe said. "I ate already. Please take the plate back."

He returned to the letters on the floor.

"You need a break, Abe."

"The settlement needs help."

"You're no good to us if you're too tired." She pressed her hands to his shoulders and started to rub. "You need to rest."

Her hands on his shoulders felt soothing. She pressed her palms into the back of his muscles where the tension built, ready to burst through his skin. When was the last time he had been touched? Hugged? Rubbed? Soothed? His coat hung by the door. He wore a thin shirt that allowed her hands to reach through the fabric with sensuality. The softness of her touch made him carve the letters with more ferocity.

"You can't do this to yourself. We need you at your best."

He turned to Kelsey once again, the point of his knife at rest in the wood shavings.

"Who's been saying that?"

"No one," she said. "After the woods—I know you're tired. If we found James we—"

"We won't!" He dropped the knife and stood up. Kelsey's head was at his chest as he stared down at her. He wanted to forget the outliers existed, that James existed, even if the memories of San Diego crept into Abe's dreams, even if the nightmares of the forest burst into life every time Abe looked at the trees. If he didn't think about them long enough they would just go away, but nightmares didn't work that way. The more he tried not to think about them the more they taunted him.

Kelsey grabbed Abe's waist. "You're safe here," she said. "You don't have to be afraid of them. They can't hurt you."

"I'm not afraid of them," he said. Kelsey was wrong. They could hurt him, they have hurt him. Her hands were firm and reassuring. She pressed her head into his chest.

"We're all here for you," she said. She kissed his body through his shirt. Her fingers held tighter to his skin beneath the clothes. "You've protected us for so long. Who's going to protect you?" She lifted his shirt and pressed her warm lips to his stomach. She stood up and kissed his neck. Her coat dangled to her knees. He lifted his arms and she took his shirt away in a swift movement.

She understood him; she knew all he wanted

was to protect everyone from the world around them—and from themselves. He was the only one who could. They had all been through perdition together. *Hell didn't have to be eternal,* he thought, *if we could crawl our way out of it.* He still felt the remnants of gasoline on his fingertips, beneath the nails, now engulfed in rotten black flesh. If he could have left bits of his flammable skin on the gates of hell, he could have blown those gates open long ago.

Kelsey's hair brushed his cheeks. She smelled of flowers, live ones. He inhaled the scent once more wanting to replace the air of decay that surrounded him too often. He wrapped his hands around her shoulders and brought her close, kissed her hard. The pressure of their lips pushed their tongues together by itself. She turned him around, pushed him onto the bed and dropped her coat. The coat made a weak whisper on the ground and covered the initials Abe had worked into the wood. With the exception of her boots, Kelsey stood only in her bra and underwear. Her hair looked fire red and he wanted to dip his hand into it to feel a burning emulsion. He pressed himself up on his elbows and watched her. She dug the toes of one foot to the heel of the other and kicked away a boot, then the other. She bit her lip and smiled. Her scent drifted from her hair to the bed. Did his sheets already smell like her?

She took a small, slow step to the bed. One leg drifted in front of the other before she made it to the edge. She had moved the coat, with a subtle flick of her naked foot, pushing it out of the way. In the dim light beyond Kelsey's legs, beneath where the coat had been, one complete "A" sat next to an unfinished "E." The letters looked back at him without the haze of wood shavings encircling the names—*their names*.

"I can't," he said.

"You just need to rest," she whispered again. She leaned toward him. Abe sat up. She reached for his lips. The familiar smell of decay replaced the newness of Kelsey's flowery scent.

"Stop," he said. "You need to get your coat and go."

"But—"

"Get your coat," he said. "And go." She grabbed the coat, quickly pressed her feet back into her boots and didn't look back. Abe sat back on the floor and outlined the depths of the unfinished initials.

"I'm sorry," he said to no one. "I couldn't protect you. I couldn't protect anyone. I can now."

The thought became resolute, the idea iron, now more than ever, that he would find the outliers. He picked up the knife.

Æ

The world had turned rotten. What if that smell wasn't the rest of the world? What if that rancid scent was his body, his mind, his past, his future? The thought felt ridiculous.

But in this world of absurdity all truths came from the ridiculous. Twisting lines emanated from his black fingertip, like a cartoon, a sign of pungency wafting up from the dead tissue. It was him—the rot rose from him, from the finger. He needed to find a way to get rid of it before he found James. Purify himself before he purified the island.

A SHADOW
IN THE WOODS

SHIA

HOWLS RAN UNDER THE LEAVES AND RUSTLED THE BRANCHES; not all of the cries sounded like dogs. In the days before the snow, Shia would be hard-pressed to have spoken out about what he liked, what he didn't like, where he thought his future would take him. He had been seven years old when the world started to die. He had grown into someone a bit bigger, a bit sadder, a lot angrier, and no longer able tell the difference between the latter two.

Sometimes he walked through the woods because he had nothing better to do. Sometimes he walked through the woods because he could shout at the top of his lungs without anyone hearing. "What if someone hears you?" a boy with round eyes and thin eyebrows once asked. "You'd get in trouble. *They* might be trouble." The settlement often spoke of the outliers like they were ghosts—of Abe like he was a god. That was when Shia decided to walk alone.

Today he walked through the woods because he feared Abe might come after him for the comments he had made about the salt. He understood if the settlement needed to ration, but Abe shouldn't complain about it, especially if he didn't have his finger on the pulse of the rations in the first place.

Shia pulled down his hood and let the cold stab at his cheeks. His hair curled around his eyebrows in dark clusters. He pushed the curls back from his face. The howls continued. Some of the calls were high-pitched. They sang in the air like memories of a troubled past. The raspy echo that accompanied the hollow howls didn't sound like a dog. Maybe that crisp call was human, filled with more than animal instinct, settled somewhere on the edge of despair, more like a scream than a howl. Since the night of the dog packs, everyone seemed on edge, if not from the attack then something else; Abe's quiet demeanor held a shell of himself. Shia didn't know why he had stayed in the first place. After such a long time of feeling like he was lied to—by adults, by other kids, by James, then by Abe—Shia started lying to himself. He stayed in the settlement because he preferred Abe to James. He stayed because when he pictured Abe, he saw the boy from Fornland: sure of himself, ready to save the world by saving them all. James was Shia's image of a lost childhood, not his own but his best friend, Marcus.

"The closest thing to brothers we'll ever know," Marcus once said. That was how the two boys felt before the snow fell. After Shia witnessed the liquor store clerk's brains splatter against the shop window, the boys drifted apart. Shia hadn't spoken to anyone about how the image haunted him. Marcus tried to get Shia to talk to James. Shia had, but it wasn't until he spoke with Abe that the dark images began to fade.

"You can get past it," Abe said. At that time it had been enough. Then Marcus never made it to the ship and Shia repeated Abe's words over and over and over, every day, every hour, until now. He finally thought he couldn't get past whatever hurdle would come next. If Shia had gone with James, maybe he wouldn't be trudging through the forest on a daily basis just to keep his mouth shut, too afraid to challenge Abe, to mention what wasn't working.

Instead of walking back to the settlement and sitting in the warm comfort of his room, Shia continued moving toward the animal cries. He wasn't sure if minutes passed or hours, but the screams continued. The forest shook and caused snow to fall from the leaves. He found two dogs stretching their snouts to the sky; their calls reverberated off the tree trunks. Between them sat Charlotte, crying her anemic call to the metallic sky. Her hood was down and her face lifted up, on her knees with her hands to her chest. She looked much thinner than when Shia had last seen her in the flickering light of the forest night. Shia stood a distance away. Charlotte stood and Shia saw the deer carcass on the ground above drops of stained snow. She was about to pick up a deer but stopped and looked at Shia, or near Shia.

Shia didn't know what Charlotte would do if she found him, but he didn't have a weapon; Charlotte had a bow. Shia lay against the tree base and pressed his face into the snow. Charlotte's steps stomped in the snow, the dogs panted, and the air turned quiet. When her body was gone, Shia decided he needed to follow her.

Footprints lasted in pure snow. Shia found where the blood trail started near Charlotte's boots. Paw prints ran around the smooth path that dragging the carcass had created. Soon Charlotte was in view. Shia wondered if he should approach her. No one in the settlement knew where the outliers hid. He would get a big reward if he found out. Maybe it would ease the anxiety that rattled his bones whenever Abe walked into a room. Maybe he could stay with the outliers instead of returning to the settlement, even if it meant having to be close to James. Which was worse, fear or anger? And how could he tell the difference anymore?

Each step Charlotte took echoed in the trees. Her sharp breaths felt close. She didn't look healthy.

If the condition of the outliers looked like that, then maybe I shouldn't even bother, he thought.

She stopped by the edge of a frozen waterway and examined the ice. A large frond had fallen and stood near the banks of the iced-over stream. She picked it up and examined it. What could she do with a dead piece of tree? She looked engrossed with the frond, touching her fingertips to its edges and turning it over and over. Shia could have spoken to her then. He could have asked to help. He could have asked for help. Instead he knelt down again, hiding behind the trees. She dug her heels into the ice. Did she want to get herself killed?

The cold started to poke at Shia's insides.

Charlotte stomped on the ice once more and then shattered the stream. She pulled at the fallen frond and reached for frozen leaves before tearing them into strips. She bound together the fronds as rope. The metallic sky sharpened. Charlotte wove a net and dragged it through the water. Maybe the outliers weren't starving at all. An occasional fish hopped out of the net and flopped onto the thin banks. When the fish landed, the dogs lunged at it, fighting each other for a superior piece until nothing was left. Charlotte had concentrated on the netting.

How much time had passed them by? He followed Charlotte to the foothills of the volcano and started to climb. She dragged the net behind her. The carcass wrapped around her shoulders, an unintended shawl. The dogs roamed behind Charlotte, occasionally snapping at the net, biting for a fish. He followed her until the trees opened up and he had nowhere to hide. She disappeared into the mountain, deer, dogs, net, and all.

The wind blew along the foothills, sweeping

from down the mountain and along the trees. Shia hadn't noticed until the chill swept over his skin. No snow fell. The wind blew often enough to keep the snow off the canopy. The leaves and branches were overrun with ice. In the midst of the open air, he decided to enter the cave. The snow was hard, empty of crunch. Shia reached the cave's mouth and saw Charlotte pass off the deer and the net now empty of fish. He stopped, unsure if he should enter completely. The dogs weren't at her side. Charlotte spoke to James and stepped away soon after.

"James," Shia said. Charlotte turned with wide eyes. Was it worry or just emaciation?

"Shia?" James asked.

"You sneaky little—" Charlotte said.

James interrupted Charlotte. "How'd you find us?"

The wind blew around him on the outskirts of the cave. Worried about the outcome, Shia decided not to enter until invited. He shouldn't have come. He shouldn't have followed Charlotte. The wind blew harder and snot ran down his upper lip, freezing to his skin. Charlotte tried to whisper but the cavernous space made every word audible.

"He followed me here." Every syllable twisted with anger.

"He's here now," James said. "It doesn't matter how."

"Get in here," James said. He reached out for Shia and pulled him inside. "It's not much, but . . ."

"It's home?" Shia asked.

"It's something," James said. He didn't take Shia deeper into the cave. It looked like everyone was too preoccupied to notice Shia at all—for the better.

"I followed—" Shia said. He looked at Charlotte. "You were—"

"That's between us and the dogs," Charlotte said.

"And the deer," Shia said.

Charlotte gave Shia a cold hard stare. "You can join it if you'd like."

"I don't think we have to worry about that," James said. The look on James's face shifted from fear to a paternal look of concern—Shia hadn't seen that look for a while. He recalled Abe giving him a similar look before he led the group to the liquor store in San Diego, but that was a look of encouragement. But every time he looked at James, he saw the reason Marcus wasn't around. Shia didn't expect it, but his words spilled out of him before he knew what he said.

"Every morning I wake up filled with fear." His cheeks ached with windburn, snot still frozen to his lip. He needed a fire but all he could see was a puff of pathetic smoke drifting in the depths of the cave. James started to speak but Shia stopped him.

"I've been filled with hate and fear since the scavs shot up the liquor store, since Marcus didn't make it out of San Diego." James didn't look away but the worry twisted to something similar to shame. "I—"

"No one was more—" James interrupted. Shia stopped him again.

"I don't want to be afraid anymore," he said. Commotion filled the depths of the cave, cheerful cries and shouts. They all sounded like animals on their last breath, in a way, like a deer grunting one last time before it dropped to the ground in the woods, except they were filled with the opposite emotion, not the dying rattle of despair but something akin to the final cheers of hope. "I don't want to be afraid."

James stayed silent and looked over Shia. He motioned him deeper into the cavern. "We're going to eat soon," James said.

"I'm not hungry," Shia said.

"Eat," James said. "Because eventually you will be."

LOOK OF BETRAYAL

CHARLOTTE

SHIA WAS THE FIRST PERSON TO FIND THE OUTLIERS ALL IN the cave, half-starved shadows of who they all were. He didn't flinch. He had joined them all for the meal. He said he wasn't hungry but the rest of the outliers knew better and encouraged him to eat.

Charlotte started to worry. *He followed me home. I put everyone in danger because I wasn't careful.* She wanted to scream again but it was her howls that put her in this mess in the first place.

She handed Shia a bowl filled with meat and water. They called it stew. The broth was thin, absent of vegetables and filled with gristly deer meat and overcooked fish that they boiled as fast as they could because hunger mattered more than flavor. Shia made faces when he ate the chewy, thick cuts of deer and dry fish but he never disparaged it. He sat quietly near the fire, unfamiliar to the unending cold the rest of them had grown accustomed to. They didn't need to stand by the meager flames in the hopes their skin would catch a touch of sobering warmth.

Charlotte watched Shia with a furrowed brow. Her eyes stung after a while. She hadn't blinked, too afraid to miss a single move Shia made. Sometimes the hardest part about the island wasn't the hunger or the cold, but the mistrust. It wasn't that she had trusted everyone in San Diego, but she couldn't think of a single moment she hadn't trusted the other kids when they all lived in the boarding-house. She could think of people she disliked, hated even. Some faces she could name while others were nothing more than empty features whose voices she recalled. She thought of the chairs and the books, the food and the vast room filled with beds where the young girls slept. The details slipped away bit by bit, but she remembered the most important details, or they became the most important details because she remembered them.

In those memories she knew kids who were afraid of others, smarter than others, but not once did she ever hear of someone mistrusting another. They had taken in Shia, the first person the outliers had even seen in months. He ate their food but spoke to no one, huddled near the fire without a second glance at anyone in the fading daylight. He had gotten close to Abe and that was enough of a reason not to trust him.

"The best food I've eaten in days," Tic-Tac said. He took a seat next to Charlotte. She kept her focus on Shia's sullen silhouette.

"It's the only food you've eaten in days," Sarah said. She sat on the opposite side of Tic-Tac.

"Doesn't make it any less true. More true even." He dug his fingers into his bowl and cupped the meat, shoving it to his mouth in swift, desperate movement. He laughed. Charlotte could feel his body pulse next to her. She had already eaten her entire bowl, as fast as she could, slurping the broth and pushing the meat to the bowl's edge, shoveling it into her mouth. She understood how Tic-Tac felt, his laughter, his desire to joke. Hunger swelled in their stomachs for too long, to the point that she had been ready to eat the frozen dirt beneath the sheets of snow, or tear the icy leaves away from the branches and gnaw on them like gum. She couldn't explain to herself why it happened, but when she took the bowl full of food she was defensive, ready to stab, claw, or bite anyone that stood between her and a meal.

As she ate, the anger and fear disappeared, replaced by giddiness. The fuller she felt, the happier she was until all the anxiety left and seemingly impossible laughter swept in. The food didn't taste better than what she had eaten in the past but it made her feel better, until the laughing stopped when Shia took his bowl and never said a word to anyone. It was a big decision to leave the settlement but he had shown up out of the blue, without her noticing, without the dogs howling. The deer had stood as a good omen, idols of refuge and safety. The fish acted as saviors. Shia was a reminder of the settlement and what Abe would do if he found the outliers. Shia was a bad omen. James may have forgiven Shia for his betrayal, how he had turned James in after Elise's death. People often forget the ripple effect of bad decisions.

Tic-Tac nudged Charlotte; she swayed but didn't budge, not from her seat and not from watching Shia.

"It's the best meal ever," Tic-Tac said. "The best meal I can remember."

Sarah giggled. Charlotte could hear the start of uncontrollable laughter setting in. If she could have held onto that feeling she would have, where she didn't feel the hurt or anxiety of life anymore. When the laughter washed over her, she felt safe from the unforgiving elements of life, like starvation. She had once again felt the comforts of friendship and the hot rush of her blushing cheeks when she smiled too hard. If she sifted through the shit long enough she would find hope once again. Tic-Tac licked his fingers. He suckled and his mouth pulled at his skin until his finger left his lips with a small pop.

"I ate too much," Tic-Tac said. "Oh, my stomach's expanding—it's moving too fast." Sarah laughed. Tic-Tac held his stomach. "I'm going into a food coma. Not a starvation-nap."

Sarah grabbed her stomach and mimicked it growing. She puffed out her cheeks.

"That's an excellent idea," she said. Her laughter was high-pitched. They sounded regal when they spoke, as if their humble stew that kept them alive was a meal made for kings and queens. Their laughter simmered around the cave. The joy was infectious, not because of their laughter, but because everyone had food and their bodies wanted a way to exalt.

"We could take on the world," Sarah said. "Take over the world."

"We already have," Tic-Tac said. Charlotte turned away from Shia. Tic-Tac held his arms around his chest. He had tears in his eyes. His cheeks flushed as he laughed, lurching back and forth. Sarah did the same in the opposite direction. They looked like they sat on opposing ends of a hilarious seesaw.

"We didn't take shit," Charlotte said. "And if that's what you think then you haven't been paying attention." She kept her voice low so Shia wouldn't hear her words echo, hoping that her words wouldn't reverberate in the cave at all and Tic-Tac and Sarah wouldn't hear them somewhere deeper than their ears.

They stopped, but the cave continued to laugh with others strewn around the grounds with full, giddy bellies. Tic-Tac wiped the tears from his cheeks. Sarah leaned on Tic-Tac's shoulder and looked at Charlotte with hurt eyes, where the hazel surrounding the irises turned to storm clouds.

"When did you lose your sense of humor?" Sarah asked.

"We're stuck in a cave, hungry and cold, and you're saying we've taken on the world? We're lucky to have made it to a piece of rock that had some sort of buoyancy left."

"Like we don't know that," Tic-Tac said. All the laughter was cleared from his voice, his face, his body. Charlotte now felt worse for stealing what could have been anyone's final laugh. Guilt could cause a downward spiral of shame that would lead nowhere good. She didn't apologize; that wouldn't bring the laughter back. "We had a second, just one second, to forget about that and you wouldn't let us have it."

"We shouldn't—" Charlotte said.

"No," Tic-Tac said. "You *couldn't*." He put his hood on and lay down with his hands over his eyes. Charlotte watched Sarah, who seemed to look at him with grace and sadness. Sarah had spoken, the quiet between her and Tic-Tac grew and spread like an icicle, popping any excess laughter in its path and leaving only silence.

Finally Charlotte broke the emptiness. "I just don't trust him," she whispered. She looked at Tic-Tac who took his hands from his eyes. "Him, I mean."

"He's been through the same thing we have," Sarah said.

"Is it because he turned James in?" Tic-Tac asked.

"No," Charlotte said. "I mean, yes. That's part of it. Would you trust him after what he did?"

"James seems to," Sarah said. "If anyone has cause to be upset, it's him not us."

"That's bullshit," Charlotte said. "We can be pissed too, you know. It pushed us out of the settlement too. I had to watch James almost die—twice. Why can't I be angry too?"

"He came to us," Tic-Tac said. "He could have

gone back to the settlement and told Abe. He didn't."

"Trust is all we have left," Sarah said.

"That's why I want to hold onto it," Charlotte said. "I don't want to give it away to . . . *him*. I don't think he's even eaten the food."

"It's a big change," Sarah said.

"We all needed time to adjust," Tic-Tac said.

"No," Charlotte said. "We didn't. If we took time, we died. Time kills."

"Maybe you need time to adjust to him," Sarah said.

The smoke from the distant, dwindling fire rose in pathetic bursts. Shia sat with his hands toward the smolder, the bowl by his side untouched. Charlotte didn't want to trust him. She didn't want to see him. She couldn't understand why James, Tic-Tac, and Sarah were so quick to forgive, so quick to trust. But in the dim glow of the dying light, she understood why they were different from her.

Charlotte had entered the boardinghouse long

after the three of them. The rules of life were different for them. They grew up with a different code, a different understanding than she had. Shia wasn't the problem now. Maybe she was.

CLINGING IMAGES

ABE

THE INFIRMARY SMELLED OF DISINFECTANT THAT THE SETTLE-
ment didn't even have, a leftover smell of
nostalgia Abe had from all the times he spent in
the hospital waiting for his parents' discharge.
The settlement had even set up the room in a similar fashion, six beds with bedframes, a cabinet for
the drugs, and as much white as they could have
stripped from the cruise ship walls to recreate the
healthcare image they had retained after all this time.

Rudy had seemed surprised to see Abe, scared
even. He had always been quiet but became more
skittish after Buck died, after he had received five
lashes. He spoke less, made less eye contact with

everyone other than Claire, and lost the humor Abe
had once found so biting.

"You still have the operator's touch?" Abe asked
when he entered the infirmary.

"He's busy," Claire had said. Whatever fear Abe
knew he struck in other kids around Fornland was
absent in Claire. She resembled a rabid dog, protecting her master while Rudy tried to appear busy.

"I didn't ask you," Abe said. He made to walk
past Claire but she stepped in his way.

"Do you have an appointment?" she asked. Her
eyepatch gave her a fierce look. Before her run-in
with the chandelier shards, she had been sweet,
small, quiet, and out of Abe's way; once she got the
eyepatch, Claire took on a different persona.

"I don't need a goddamned appointment," Abe
said. "Do I Rudy?"

"Everyone needs an—"

"It's okay," Rudy said. Claire turned back to him.
Rudy stopped pretending to make the beds. Abe
walked over to Rudy and Rudy flinched.

"What do you need?" Rudy asked.

"A quick fix," Abe said.

"Then you're in the wrong place," Rudy said. "A quick fix could kill you. Look at our parents. Look at Buck—" Rudy recoiled at the sound of Buck's name, lost in a way to the same drug that took his parents.

"I didn't mean drugs."

"Of course you didn't."

Abe took off his gloves with his teeth. Claire watched over the mattress, ready to defend Rudy at any second. *Like a loyal guard dog*, Abe thought. When Abe's glove came off, the rotten smell of his finger returned. The smell probably filled his glove, stained the fabric. Abe didn't hide the dead muscle and tissue tainting his index finger.

"Frostbite," Rudy said. "I've never seen it this bad."

"How bad is it?" Abe asked.

"You want to sit?" Rudy asked.

"No," Abe said. He held his gloves in his other hand.

"You see that green and yellow outline around the black skin?" Rudy pointed to the border colors and brushed Abe's hand. Abe half-expected a vindictive pressure placed on his finger and braced himself for the pain Rudy would pursue, but it never came. Rudy was enthralled with Abe's finger. "I've never seen it this bad before. Does it hurt?"

"Only when you touch the green."

Rudy leaned in closer and scrunched his nose.

"How long has it been this way?" He scrunched his nose again. "Doesn't even matter. However long is too long. It smells funky."

"What do you say, Doctor? And you can stay out of it," Abe said to Claire.

"You're finger needs to be cut off."

"What makes you say that?"

"Before that green and yellow area has a chance to spread. It's a bacteria, infecting and destroying your tissue. Claire, get the iron."

Claire left the room without hesitation.

"How do I know I can believe you?" Abe asked.

"You don't," Rudy said.

"That's the Rudy I know and love."

"You should sit," Rudy said. Abe continued to stand. "Sit, *now*." Abe took a seat at the edge of the mattress. Rudy searched the room for an extra towel and found one, rolled it up, and handed it to Abe. "When I tell you, put this in your mouth, between your teeth." Rudy pulled a sturdy table up to Abe. "Place your hand here, palm down."

"What's going—" Abe started to say.

"Do it," Rudy interrupted.

Abe obliged. Rudy had a look of determination, a sadistic stare filled with focus. It exhilarated Abe a little. Claire returned with a knife glowing orange, freshly placed in a fire.

"What's that for?" Abe asked.

"You're about to find out if I still have my surgeon's hands."

"Knives aren't allowed out of the kitchen," Abe said.

"They are for medical emergencies," Claire said.

"This is an emergency?" Abe asked. Claire and Rudy nodded. Rudy stood and held Abe's wrist against the table. The knife flickered with heat.

"The heat disinfects the steel. It also helps cut through bone like butter. You remember butter, real butter, don't you?"

"My dad always said real butter was like heroin," Abe said.

"Our parents would know," Rudy said. "Grab that towel and shove it between your teeth." Abe did as he was told. Sweat poured from his forehead. It was the hottest he had been since summer in San Diego when he had run away from Fornland.

"Ready?" Abe mumbled through the towel.

"Help hold him," Rudy told Claire. She placed her hands on Abe's arm to hold his hand steady. Abe swore Rudy took pleasure from this, revenge for the lashes, for Buck, but Rudy never should have hidden that his best friend stole and used the settlement's morphine.

"Do it!" Abe yelled through the towel. He

already clenched. Rudy took the blade and sliced through Abe's index finger, close to the knuckle to cut out the spread of gangrene. The pain was unbearable. Abe wanted to pass out. He clenched the rough towel in his teeth and bit down. The heat made his skin bubble, then the blade cut his flesh, struck the bone, carved the bone, and created dust. He heard the sound of the knife sawing through his skin and the bone coming apart, and then the heat returned, cauterizing the wound near the knuckle, above the pool of blood on the tray. Abe twitched and convulsed. Claire held him tighter. The decay left Abe's nostrils, the rot cut away from his wound. Covered in an ocean of his own sweat near the collected sanguine that poured from his body, he felt more whole without the finger than he had with it. He lay down on the bed, Claire still holding his arm.

"You still have those surgeon hands, Rudy," Abe said. He took a deep breath.

"I'll get you some medicine," Rudy said.

"No," Abe said. "I'm fine."

"You just had your finger cut off," Rudy said.

Claire let go of Abe's forearm.

"Good riddance," Abe said.

THE DIFFERENCE
IN SURVIVAL

JAMES

JAMES TRIED TO GET SHIA TO TALK TO HIM. SHIA SAT HUD-
dled with his legs wrapped in his arms,
shaking slightly from the cold, and staring at the
subtle smolder of timber and weak smoke that
came to define the fires in the cave. Shia hadn't
known what he gave up until it was gone. James
understood Shia must miss the luxuries of the
settlement, things that he hadn't known were luxuries until he left them behind.

"It's a tough spot you're in," James said. "You'll
survive. We have. You said it yourself: you don't
want to be afraid anymore. You don't have to be
afraid here." As soon as James said it he realized

he had lied. Shia didn't need to fear Abe or the settlement. He didn't need to fear dogs or drowning. What they all feared, with the exception of at that moment, what everyone in the cave woke up worried about, James had noticed, was that they were starving to death and soon they wouldn't be lucky enough to have one last meal, or worse, they wouldn't be lucky enough to die quickly.

"Take it," Shia had said. He pushed the bowl closer to James.

"You need to eat," James said.

"I don't want it."

"It's not about want, Shia."

James stared at the bowl. He almost reached for it. He had to pull his fingers back and keep his arms behind him. Even if he was full now, he wanted to pour that stew down his throat, because he didn't know when he would feel this again. He didn't know when his body would be nourished— his mind nourished. He couldn't take that bowl. It wasn't his to take.

"It is to me."

If Shia wouldn't eat it then someone else would have to. Waste was a word that went out with the warm weather.

James waved over Teagan. The smile loomed large along Teagan's cheeks.

"Anyone sick?" James asked.

"Sick?" Teagan asked. "No one's sick."

"Who's the thinnest?"

"The thinnest? On purpose?"

"Who's the biggest?"

"The biggest?" Teagan echoed. "Tic-Tac, I think."

"I think you're right. Quietly run this over to Tic-Tac." James handed Teagan the bowl with his finger over his lips. "Just say someone didn't need it." He watched as Teagan ran the bowl to Tic-Tac who shoveled the stew without a second thought. James noticed Shia turn from the wood. Tic-Tac cupped the meat, slurped the water, and dropped the bowl to the ground. He lay down looking exhausted afterwards, as if eating was the most tiring activity he could have done.

Shia's eyes burned dark brown and pierced James. Too many thoughts swirled through James's mind to count, to hold onto even. They flew one after the other until he grabbed onto a firm word.

"Whether you forgive me for Marcus or not, I understand, but I don't hold a grudge," James said.

Shia turned back to the fire and didn't say another word. James's stomach gurgled, happy for the food but angry it didn't have more. He couldn't have eaten that extra bowl if he had wanted to. The food wasn't James's to eat. The rest of the outliers were as starved as he was. It wouldn't have been right to take the food. Now in the darkness he wanted to hold onto Charlotte. When the light started to peek through the mouth of the cave, he wouldn't be happy or full. He would be hungry once more.

CHARLOTTE

Charlotte had wanted to coax the truth from Shia before he had a chance to betray them all. He had sat in the waning light and cozied up to James by offering his food, even though James was too smart to accept it. She couldn't let this person, who had already turned them inside out once, do it again. She had to show them all what Shia's motives were, to save them all—to save herself—to show that her distrust was justified. She had tried to talk to James, Sarah, and Tic-Tac. Charlotte tried to make them all understand that things changed when Shia arrived.

"Hear me out," Charlotte had said. "If we go to him first we can straighten it all out. We can get some leverage."

"We should have leverage before we go," Sarah said.

"Why go at all?" James asked. "We ate today. We had more today than in weeks. You found a way to catch fish. We can stay."

"What about the cold?" Tic-Tac asked. "What if the weather gets worse and the deer start to die?"

"You too now?" James asked.

"This isn't a long-term plan here," Charlotte said. "And it's already been months."

"And how can we get back in? You think he's just going to welcome us back with open arms? He tried to kill me. He tried to strangle Tic-Tac. This guy's going to let us walk back in there?"

"What about us?" Sarah asked.

"She's right," Charlotte said. "What about the rest of them that he might allow back?"

"That's not what I meant," James said.

"What did you mean?" Sarah asked. "You'd rather let us all stay out here until it's too late?"

"I didn't say that."

"I don't know, man," Tic-Tac said. "If we have a chance, shouldn't we take it? If not for us, for them?"

"Maybe we should sleep on this," James said. "For a day or two. Until we figure out some leverage."

Most of the outliers settled in for the night, snuggled up against one another or wrapped in their own arms close to some of the embers that never died but looked like they soon would. Shia continued to stare at the little flicker of orange that fed the smoke. His eyes barely moved from that spot since he arrived. It served him through the cold and the heat. Charlotte took his lack of response as arrogance.

Charlotte sat next to him in the same spot James had sat earlier. He had tried to coax Shia to eat, wanted to spoon-feed him understanding and hope. Charlotte wanted to do the opposite. If the air smelled enough of decay and imminent death, maybe Shia would leave them alone, return to the settlement without giving them up. She would fill him with thoughts that the outliers would all perish soon anyway.

"You cold?" Charlotte asked. For once she meant the question, as opposed to when it rose up as a hello. The longer the outliers stayed in the cave, listening to the wind and watching the ice reshape over the landscape night after night, the more they felt like their blood grew thicker and the cold didn't hit as hard. *Some feelings people aren't supposed to get used to*, she thought.

Shia shook his head, pressing his legs closer to his chest and digging his chin into his knees.

"You'll get used to it," she said. She needed to make him feel comfortable to bring out the truth. If she didn't hear it, she wanted to see it, in his eyes or his body language, somewhere that would give away his cowardice and intent. "The rest of us have." The words sounded casual when she said them aloud but in her head they burned with accusation. She wanted to say it again with the same vitriol that lingered in her thoughts. The rest of the outliers didn't want to get used to the cold, away from the heated rooms of the settlement; they had to. Even the ones that ran away. Shia didn't deserve that same sense of comfort. He didn't deserve the ability to cope.

"You sure about that?" he asked.

He didn't elaborate. Did he question whether everyone was used to the cold or whether he would be there long enough to accept it? At times Charlotte took comfort in it. When no one was watching she would step outside before sunrise and take off her coat, for a second or two, until the cold air made the goose bumps rise over her body. The hungrier she felt, the more often she did it, but not because it diminished the hunger. If anything it added to it, the knowledge that her body ate itself alive, that any fat she had left on her body could count down until it disappeared with the rest of her. The continued discomfort from the hunger pains, the cold, at moments she may have forgotten, or at times her body tired out, blanketed in exhaustion, she wanted to strip down to nothing and remind herself that she wasn't dead yet. She never asked Shia to explain himself.

"You didn't eat," she said.

"You on me about that now too?"

"Not even close," she said. Shia's dark brown eyes widened.

The fire didn't add any color or glint to the iris. They could have made the fire bigger, to give them a little more light and heat. Charlotte knew Shia thought it because she had thought the same thing once. But the fire needed to stay low. They kicked up the flames when they had food, otherwise they couldn't afford to let too much smoke fill the cave, or worse, leave the cave and signal the settlement.

"What is it then?" he asked.

"What's the problem?" she asked. "Your problem."

"I don't have a problem."

"You came here, sat down, and haven't moved since. You didn't eat and said barely anything all day. What's *your* problem?" Tic-Tac snored and the familiar murmur rattled Charlotte's cheeks. Some people found it to be a comfort. Whether through familiarity or constant sound, Charlotte counted herself among those that thought it soothing. It filled the uncomfortable void between her and Shia when instead of talking she wanted to reach over and shake him until he admitted his plan, his faults, or until his head fell off his neck.

"He didn't take it," Shia said. The lack of flicker in his eyes turned watery, holding back tears.

Who didn't take what? Charlotte thought. *Abe didn't take the bait?*

"James didn't take the food."

It had been a test? Shia tested James with the food, set up to fail, and passed? What kind of test was it when Shia looked upset and surprised about the outcome? Could that be my cue, Shia's disappointment in how James responded to the food?

"He wasn't hungry," Charlotte lied. Everyone was hungry, always. Some nights she couldn't tell if the rumble pushing against the walls was Tic-Tac's snores or the group's stomachs rumbling at once. The lie came out thin and Shia knew it.

"You're all hungry," he said. Shia looked at her now with the full force of teary eyes that dammed around the irises, magnifying the color but stuck there, not allowed to flood. "He gave it away. Would you have given it away?"

"Of course I—"

"Tell the truth," Shia said. The words hit Charlotte like an explosion. When the truth was ugly, she didn't want to look at it; she would rather think of the lies with which she would convince herself. The biggest lie at that moment: she would have given away the food. "You're going to look me in the eye and tell me that, even if you had just finished an entire bowl, you wouldn't have eaten mine? How bad did you want to knock someone else over and steal theirs? You wanted more for yourself and less for them."

Charlotte forced the "no" from between her teeth. "I wouldn't have taken anyone's food."

"But—"

"I wouldn't have given yours away."

"You don't know how much time I spent angry at James for letting Marcus die. I hated him for it—so much it made me afraid. I don't know. At some point it became so strong I could taste it . . . some flavor between rotten and whatever's worse than that."

"What's worse?"

"I don't know. Decay, maybe. I clung to Abe because of it. I thought he would save us all. He had, in a way. And I thought he still would. I thought he would keep us all going. He slipped somewhere along the line. I thought he was the compassionate one—the understanding one. But he wouldn't have given away the food."

"You don't get it," Charlotte said.

"No," Shia said. "I don't."

"No one would have given it away. No one except James. And you forced him out here. What comes next?"

"I was wondering the same thing. I felt your eyes on me all night."

"Not hard to watch you when you're by the only fire we have."

"Not what I meant."

"I know what you meant. Count on that feeling."

"He gave the food away," Shia mumbled to himself in defeated breaths. Charlotte stood up. The glow of the fire flickered smaller. She threw an extra log on the tiny flames.

"It'll kick up in a minute, maybe last an hour. Enjoy it while you can." When she walked away the pit started to crackle. The smoke drifted a little heavier. Shia stayed with his arms wrapped over his knees. Tic-Tac continued to snore and the deep roar bounced off of the rocky walls. Shia didn't say what Charlotte hoped he would say. He didn't admit to a future betrayal, but she couldn't dismiss that it would come soon. She had to do something to protect James, herself, all of them. She had to do something.

ALWAYS
IN THE NIGHT

JAMES

IT WAS DARK IN THE CAVE WHEN JAMES FELT THE LIGHT TOUCH of Charlotte rub against him. They had spent enough time together that he knew her touch, the sound of her breath, the little expulsion of hot air in the cave's cold, even down to the way her breath smelled after she ate, or lately, after she hadn't eaten. But tonight they had food in their stomachs and smiles on their faces. While everyone else seemed carefree, James worried their joy would echo out of the opening and lead Abe right to them. A stupid thought, he knew, but sometimes for James joy and fear were inseparable.

Charlotte tried to press her body closer to James's

but there was already no space between them. He wrapped his arm around her and felt comforted by her scent, that specific aroma no one seemed to have but her, from the way the natural oils settled in her hair, pressed on her skin, to the way her sweat mixed with the deteriorating fabric of her clothes, it all led to a deeper understanding of her. More than that, her hair had lost all sense of the white color that once covered every strand. It now dangled closer to her belly button than to her scalp. He knew more about her than just her circular green eyes and believed he now saw deeper than the green, where the color merged with the things she carried inside her: the past, the present, and hopeful emotions that came with thoughts of a future.

"What time is it?" he asked. Time was referential to the light. They no longer wondered about specific hours but wanted to know about how dark the night looked, how many stars shined, if the moon lingered, or where the sunlight happened to be at the time. When James asked about the time it struck him as curious because he hadn't fallen asleep with Charlotte, as usual, and now that she pressed her body against his to stay warm in the depths of the cave, his curiosity about where she might have been and at what time he might have fallen asleep kept him awake.

"It's dark," she said.

"How dark?" he asked.

"No moon," she said. "Go back to sleep."

He wrapped his arm around her waist. With a full stomach—the first in days—most of the others found it easy to fall asleep anywhere. Even James felt sleepy after his fit of laughter, which acted like a soothing drug.

"Where were you?" James asked.

"Couldn't sleep," she said.

"But now?"

"I'll get there. You first, though."

He felt the slow rhythms of her breath as she drifted into dreaming. She probably had gone for a walk around the foothills. Sometimes she would look for any semblance of the Northern Lights, James knew. She said they soothed her when she couldn't sleep but they hadn't been around for a long time. Her voice and body had been tense since Shia arrived.

James remembered trying to make Shia feel welcome, to show that there were no hard feelings about what Shia had done. Most of the lives they had all lived in San Diego had shed away like old skin, but James tried hard to hold onto some semblance of their past, even if in principle, and one of those principles was trust. He wanted to trust Shia and in order to do that James needed Shia to know that he forgave him.

ABE

The lights of the settlement had gone out long ago, but Abe wanted to watch the starlight drift over the mountain. The volcano had once held a sense of hope for everyone when they first arrived on the island. Birdcalls and hot pools told them they could survive. In their harsh reality, the island let them survive. Abe couldn't look at it any other way and it made him angrier and angrier. The earth let them survive. The settlement—Abe, James, Elise—had little to do with it. When he watched the enormity of the stars in the night, amassed by a collection of swirled light, the individual stars became insignificant. Individuals didn't matter. Their light faded too quickly. Individuals couldn't add enough color or shine to illuminate the dark, but together they all could.

He pressed his fingers against the faded scars of his and Elise's initials on the doorframe. He would have to go over it again soon. Dig deep enough for the outline not to weaken. He opened the door and the heat escaped. It was his favorite moment of the day, when the comfort of his room came to greet him like an excited puppy, rushing out of the cracked door, brushing his cheeks. Except a different scent emanated from the inside, familiar but distant, one he knew but couldn't place, almost tasted, lingering at the edge of his tongue, against the outside of his lips. He didn't pause for long but when he closed the door he remembered where he had smelled that mixture of sweat and fear, ice and death.

"All I have to do is say the word," Abe said.

"It's me," Shia said. His voice hung in the darkness, strained and insecure. In the outline of the light that beamed through the window, Abe saw Shia's silhouette in the far corner. He tucked himself against the wall and hid in the shadows.

"What are you doing skulking over there?" Abe asked. "I thought you were . . . someone else."

"I didn't want anyone to see me," Shia said.

"Why not?"

"I didn't know if you would want me back after—"

Abe stood by the door, his back against the

wood. He had imagined Charlotte standing in the corner with an arrow pulled back taut and ready to let loose. He would stand against the wall ready for the single blow of the solitary firing squad to enter his chest. In the shade of the bed, he saw his and Elise's initials consecrating the floor. Every day when he woke up, before he went to bed, when he stood or stayed in his room—it didn't matter—he would look at the initials and miss her more and more, struggling to understand the darkness she saw when she decided to die, but never quite seeing the light they had made together. But it wasn't Charlotte at all. Shia had come in from the cold.

"Sit," Abe said. "Somewhere other than the floor." Shia stood up and never took another seat. Abe walked to the bed and sat down.

"We need to talk," Shia said.

"Naturally," Abe said. "Why else would you be here?"

The smell of fear almost overpowered Abe. It filled up the room, a backed-up sewer of shitty emotion that Abe loathed. It poured off Shia as if he bathed in it and it started to pool at his feet. *What caused Shia to sneak around in the darkness? What had he done that warranted secrecy and caused fear? Had Shia ever killed anything, a deer even? He had led the expedition out of San Diego that got Marcus killed. Had he ever taken responsibility for that, accepted the blame, or did he still carry the torch and point it at James?* Abe didn't take pride in the people he killed, or the fact that he had killed at all, but he took pride in knowing he did what needed to be done. He took responsibility for what had to be done. Could Shia do that? He never released a bow into someone or something. Shia sat comfortably in the committee, quiet and respectful but not ever proactive. He couldn't have come to kill Abe, not even if Abe had let him.

"I'm glad you're not here to kill me," Abe said.

"How do you know that?" Shia asked.

"If you were you would have done it already. Why, are you?" Abe laughed. It felt good to laugh, even if it wasn't real. It put Shia at enough ease to be able to say whatever he had to say. It took the anxiety out of the room, at least for a moment. Shia's face caught the light—not his entire face, but his cheeks. They were rosy and chubby. Pale had long ago become the look of everyone, no matter their original skin tone—black, white, brown, pasty, dark, red, orange—there would always be some pigment missing, but Shia's skin took on a different type of pale, an unhealthy pale that came from fear. It came from a cowardly glow that emanated from his stomach. It came from weakness.

"The outliers want to come back," Shia said.

"I'm not keeping them out," Abe said.

"They want to come back," Shia said. He hadn't meant to burst the sentence. Abe could tell by Shia's reaction to his own voice.

"From the look of you, I didn't know if you still had any spice left in you."

"What do you mean?"

"How do you know they want back in?"

"What do you mean by spice?"

"Shia, focus. You came to tell me something. How do you know they want back in?" The light through the window focused in on Shia's cheeks. They seemed more round than when he was younger. He had grown taller, but his youth showed in his face.

"I—" Shia said.

"You what?" Abe asked. "They all look like they're doing fine out there on their own. They could have come back whenever they wanted to. Their being out there doesn't affect us."

"I found them," Shia said. The thought of the outliers made Abe cringe, not because they fled from the settlement, but because they reminded him of his own failure, that he was an insignificant star. The outliers' existence meant Abe couldn't pull the light together and guide them all into some semblance of a life away from the past, filled with forgetfulness, emptiness, superfluousness, anger, and dread. They would become nothing more than what they had always been, disposable. If the outliers returned, they could all try again; they could reshape the settlement and push forward into a united galaxy.

It was harder to admit the greenhouse wasn't producing. Since Teagan left, Abe couldn't measure the amount of meat the new butcher trashed by hacking away at the bones and sinew of perfectly good deer. It was all a waste and Charlotte caused it. She protected James. Without him no one ever would have left. Charlotte wouldn't have left—the greenhouse wouldn't be dying. James was the reason the settlement wouldn't survive long if the outliers didn't come back. And the more Abe thought about James, the more James became expendable.

"How?" Abe asked.

"I tracked them," Shia said.

"You've always been a terrible liar," Abe said.

"I heard—found—Charlotte in the woods hunting this morning. I followed her." Abe tried to catch a glimpse of Shia's eyes in the shadows. It was hard to tell what people really thought, but it wasn't hard to tell when they lied. He hadn't hunted a day since they came to the island—at least, he hadn't hunted for any food.

"You don't look too good," Abe said. "You feeling okay? You eat some of their tainted meat or something? Is that it? They're half of what they used to be? They need food? Maybe James isn't taking care of them like he promised he would?"

"They aren't doing so well, but James is—"

"He's what?" Abe asked.

"He's doing the best he can. They don't have much food and everyone looks miserable. I think they'd be safer here."

"Of course they would be. This is the safer place to be."

"I think they're scared."

"Do you know what fear is?" Abe stood up and stepped toward Shia. "I mean, do you really know what fear is?" The stench falling off of Shia's body was putrid. It came faster and harder the moment Abe stood up. "Are you afraid of me, Shia?"

"No," Shia said, a slight tremor in his voice.

"I don't believe you. After all we've been through, you're afraid of me."

"You had me lead everyone to the harbor in San Diego. You believed in me."

"And now you're afraid to be in the same room with me. I wonder if you know what real fear is. To wake up every day and wonder if you should just let it all go. Questioning whether it's even worth it anymore. Is it? What do you think?"

"I've seen the way they look. They're afraid they won't even have food by morning." Shia's hands shook. The reek filled the room. Abe hoped it wouldn't seep into the sheets. "When was the last time you looked at a bunch of people who didn't know when their next meal would be?" Shia asked. "Or who followed you because they believed you knew a better way? They thought you could save them, but you were really just scared and trying to save yourself?"

"Every day," Abe said. "Maybe you were a little too young to be put on the committee, if you're filled with all that fear left over from ages ago."

"No! I've been doing my job."

"Have you? You haven't told me where they are."

"Maybe they can survive out there."

"If you thought that, you wouldn't have come to me." Abe took off his gloves. The heat made the space where his index finger used to be tingle. "A phantom finger," Rudy had called it. Abe would randomly feel it now and again.

"What happened to your finger?"

"I had to take care of the rot," Abe said. "Sometimes the only way to do that is to cut it out."

"I just wanted to help them," Shia said.

"Then tell me where they are. You want them back as much as I do. You're worried for them. That's valiant of you. That's the sign of a leader, someone who cares about everyone around them."

"I want to make sure they're safe."

"Then tell me where they are."

"Not just from out there," Shia said.

Abe stared at Shia. Shia looked over the floor made of hallowed initials. In the space of compulsions and obsessive thoughts of the past, Abe felt the most judged now, in his own room, looking over the residual carvings he tried to etch into their world. Shia looked up fast from the ground as if hiding what he had seen.

"You want this to end," Abe said. Shia nodded. The longer Shia spent in the room the more pathetic Abe thought him. The stench was so rigid Abe could taste it in the back of his throat. "I want this to end too. Tell me where they are and it all ends."

"Pardon them," Shia said.

"Excuse me?"

"Promise me you'll pardon them and I'll tell you where they are."

If he pardoned everyone it would usurp his authority. If he didn't promise to pardon everyone the outliers would linger at the fringes of the settlement and his thoughts like a maggot behind his eye, eating way at the dead flesh and blurring his vision.

"Please. I need to hear it."

"What's with all this newfound fancy for James?"

"He . . . you wouldn't understand."

"Try me." The walls moved slowly with the drifting light of the stars, but the floor showed the faded initials that looked more like cracks needing repair.

"He gave his food away," Shia said.

"That makes him a fucking hero?"

"No," Shia said. "But it made him better." Shia's eyes turned blank and sullen without a trace of fear. The smell subsided and the conversation felt like a memory. Abe laughed. He tried to hold it back but it fell out, uncontrollable and sincere. The first real laugh in ages; he didn't want it to stop. If it could linger a little while longer, the pure joy that didn't come often enough anymore, the stars could shine a little brighter.

"Fine," Abe said. "All pardoned."

"Really?"

"You don't trust me?"

"I just didn't think—"

"Exactly," Abe said. "You didn't think. Now, your part of the bargain."

Shia told Abe where the outliers hid. It looked like the shadows followed Shia around. When Abe thought the light would shine over Shia's face or shoulders, the darkness crept back over him.

"I should go," Shia said.

"What's the hurry?" Abe asked. "You don't have to go back there. They'll come home and you can spend the night in your room, comfortable."

"But what if they notice I'm gone?"

"Then they'll praise you for bringing them home."

When Shia walked out the door, the smell went with him. He walked to his room and disappeared behind the buildings. Abe didn't realize that his coat had been on the entire time. Sweat dripped from his forehead and the scent of ice returned. The stars shined brightly, enough light to guide Abe to the cave. He put on an extra layer of clothes, left his gloves behind, counted to one hundred to make sure Shia was gone, and made his way into the forest.

ERUPTING WORDS

JAMES

ON THE ISLAND, THE SUN ROSE AND SET LIKE ANY OTHER place in the world, but the hours and minutes had fallen away. Time stood in increments of day and night; that was it now, the light or the darkness. Between the light and the dark, James used to hide away—not cowering, but not wanting to be a part of the world he saw in the daytime. In San Diego the daylight was filled with the life he never could grasp and the ghosts that filled the empty apartment of his childhood. He had dug his nose in books to forget about the world he didn't want to be in, to transport him to a world where he could be happy. Somewhere between the night and the day he forced himself to lead. He couldn't pinpoint the moment, if it had been a single moment at all.

If James closed his eyes in the empty minutes of the cave, he would have had a hard time knowing what time in his life it was. How long would he be here? Sweat accumulated in tiny droplets on his cheeks. It felt like the last time he had sat in the settlement waiting for judgment, except he had been half-naked then, his bruised body dragged from his room and rushed through the snow. Even in the crushing consistency of cold, James remembered how it felt for the tops of his feet to smear against the snow's surface while two boys pulled him from his room to the cell. In the vast space at the mouth of the cave the silhouette of trees made the expanse claustrophobic. Life was a matter of balance and the scales never settled near even.

"I hope you're comfortable," Abe said. He appeared out of the tree line. He held his hands over his head, the universal sign of submission and peace. His hands were dark in the night but something wasn't right; a part of Abe was lacking, missing. His index finger was gone, the festering black pointer tinted with green. It either fell off or worse. James could imagine Abe taking a knife to his own finger, trying to cut out the physical embodiment of his own weakness, a symbol of Abe's black heart.

The scent of boiled deer meat and fish continued to drift out of the cave. James's stomach didn't just rumble, it almost lurched forward after the phantom aroma, but the scent wouldn't fill his stomach any more than wishes and dreams could. He had eaten a meal already that day, but his body didn't care. Part of his body felt empty, still struggling from the days when he hadn't eaten, hoarding each bite, the gristle, the sinew, any bone or string. What James had hidden was how he had eaten through the fish bones, had sucked out any lingering meat or nutrients before licking his fingers dry.

"I expected to see myself in ashes or some deadly fast hands the next time I saw you," James said. He would never forget how Abe had made him plunge a knife into another boy's chest. Maybe hope had created a more dynamic image of what their next meeting would look like. James hadn't expected to see Abe here, but at the same time wasn't surprised. "I should've tidied up the place," James said.

"Don't tell me you didn't get my message." Abe said. "I wanted to give you a fair warning."

"Guess this place isn't the only thing that hasn't changed."

Abe put his hands down and stepped onto the plateau, closer to James, but he was careful not to approach. No matter how much James wanted to remain calm in Abe's presence, his heart almost exploded out of his chest. Abe reached into his pocket.

"Careful," James said. He stood up straight, ready to strike, run, or yell for help. Abe pulled his hand out. He held a baggie with a deer steak in it. He threw it to James's feet.

"I didn't know we had any bags," James said. He held himself back from reaching for the steak. It was a game of mind over matter, but his mind was weak because he didn't have enough of what mattered.

"We only took a few," Abe said. "For special occasions. I brought it for you."

James reached for it and opened the bag, ripped out the steak, and didn't bother taking off his gloves. He used the bag like a wrapper. He dug his fingers around the steak and tore at the meat. It had sweetness to it that he couldn't place and didn't care. It could have been made out of a shoe sole or an old tire, he would have eaten it either way—and savored every bite. He tore away chunks of deer and shoveled the smaller pieces into his mouth. In the absence of time James didn't know how fast he had eaten; he was still hungry, and Abe stood there looking at him as if James were a caged animal. He dropped the bag. A silent crinkle settled between them and dissipated as the bag blended into the snow.

"That hunger never stops," Abe said. "Does it?"

"Why'd you come?" James asked.

"I can only imagine how it must have been up in there. How hungry you all are."

"You haven't done it. You can't imagine it."

Abe sat down within arm's reach of James. If James wanted he could have pulled Abe to him, slammed his head against the rocky outcrop; rammed his fist into Abe's face. But he didn't.

"Love what you've done with yourself," James said wiggling his fingers. Abe scoffed, a stupid smirk rotting on his face, worse than his finger.

"It's just you and me up here. No one waiting for me down below. No one sneaking around the wings."

James took a long look at Abe. He didn't care what Abe would find hidden in his eyes. He didn't care how he would be read, his body language or his thoughts. He couldn't look away.

"Since when have you been so mistrusting? That used to be the only thing we counted on, remember? What had you said? Trust easy and often?"

"That would have gotten us all killed or abducted if I had said that."

"Right. It was . . . trust always but skeptically. Which if you ask me sounds pretty contradictory."

"I didn't ask you. It got us through Fornland."

"It worked out. Why don't you stick to that motto now?"

"Because I've seen what you do."

"I'm not sure what you mean, 'what I do.' I made a home for us, James. For all of us. You were a part of it once. Have you forgotten? That fear of survival disappeared for a minute there."

"Not for all of us."

"You've been out here a long time, James. A lot of them have been with you for the haul. You don't get it, do you? After going this long without a good night's sleep, without a full stomach, without some sense of civilization—hell—without a toilet for Christ's sake, is it so illogical they would be happy from two simple gestures: heat and food?"

"I think they all left for a reason," James said.

"And once they get over the indulgence of warmth and a full stomach, they'll remember why they left in the first place."

"That's the difference between you and them, I think. You have goddamned principles. You always have. You remember that time Kevin Summers beat the shit out of you?"

"Kind of hard to forget. Even in this mess of a place, that memory hasn't exactly gone away."

"You didn't tell anyone. Of course, everyone knew what happened and who had done it, but *you* kept it to yourself."

"That was Fornland. We lived that life."

"You lived that life. Anyone else would have rolled over Kevin like a Lincoln Log and suffocated him while they were at it. You came up with these rules no one else understood—no one else followed them but you. Now you're here and you're telling me you don't understand why we needed to follow the rules."

"You made them," James said.

"And you agreed to them. When did you say anything about whether or not they worked? I didn't ask for your opinion. You've gone through most of your life blaming other people for the shit that happened without ever once looking at what you did."

"And what did I do?"

"Exactly," Abe said. "What did you do?" Abe shoved his hands into his pockets. Steam rose off his cheeks.

"I didn't do anything!" James said. He was tired of Abe's voice. Every word turned into a screech that made James angrier, poking at some nerve, always poking. He wanted to be alone.

"You didn't do anything. You made a choice, as did I. I chose to do something. You chose to do nothing. It still makes you accountable for what you didn't do and could have done. That will always be your trouble; you think doing nothing means you aren't to blame for how the world works when in fact you're just as much a part of the problem."

"You could have told me this later," James said.

"Like when you're standing over my bloody corpse or something."

Abe took out a photo and handed it to James. The last photo he had seen was of Charlotte's parents. She used to carry it with her in San Diego. It had blown up with the ship. The photo had been stuffed in their cabin on the cruise ship. James was supposed to go back for it. He would have too, if the photo hadn't been burned to ash by the explosion. When he had told her, she didn't want to leave the room for almost two days. "It's like losing them all over again," she said. James didn't know anyone had photos left. He figured all the photos anyone may have smuggled out of San Diego suffered the same fate as Charlotte's. Abe waved it in his fingers.

James took it. The gloss stuck to his greasy gloves. The photo was crinkled and worn. The colors had faded. James didn't know who had taken the picture. He didn't remember the photo but he remembered the moment. He stood on the pier with Tin Fish restaurant in the background. James even remembered the smell of fried seafood and the salty air around them. Abe had James in a headlock but they both smiled. Elise stood by Abe's side with her hand roughly running through his hair. James could hear the waves crashing on the shore as he looked at the photo. He felt the warm sun on his shoulders and the smile so big it hurt his cheeks. He couldn't remember why he laughed, which now hurt a little. He could too often remember the reasons he had been sad in his lifetime but not enough reasons why he laughed, or laughed so hard he cried, but he could remember that they happened. This photo was proof.

"I haven't forgotten," Abe said. "I never will."

"Neither will I. But—"

"It doesn't have to be this way," Abe said.

Abe sat up straight. His stare became intense, focused on James to the point he could feel it.

"Just say you've made a mistake. It all goes back to normal. I know what people think of me. But I know what they think of you too. If you come back the past goes away, like it never happened, and we can all move forward."

James slipped the photo back to Abe along the frosty ground. He couldn't do it. He hadn't been wrong. He couldn't surrender to what he didn't believe in. Abe took it. His eyes turned soft, then to steel, then to fire.

"It doesn't have to be this way!" Abe said.

"It already is this way," James said. For the same reasons he didn't give up Kevin Summers, he wouldn't give up himself. For the same reasons Abe wanted James to admit fault, James couldn't. Some people don't have principles while others die for theirs. Abe was right; James spent too long not making decisions because he didn't want to be at fault. It didn't change history, it didn't change lives, but it still shaped their future. This time James made a decision to act.

Abe stood up. The nostalgia in his voice had shifted to anger.

"The greenhouse is dying," Abe said. He wore the familiar shade of sorrow.

"The real reason you want us back?" James asked.

"The reason we need you back. They want to see you."

"No," James said. "I don't." He coughed. His body felt weak despite the food he'd been given. Too little too late, he imagined. His body had gained and lost so much weight since he got to the island. Fevers burned and broke. His muscles ached and soothed. But the cough never left and he felt the blood start to pool in his lungs. He swore he could hear it swish around his organs when he moved.

Abe's eyes cast over the ground. James wanted to reach out. How could this person have become a monster? It didn't matter now. This was where they were and what they had become.

"I can't do it anymore."

"I always thought you were the smart one," Abe said. "It doesn't take courage to die. It takes courage to live." The words filled the distance between them.

"What happened to us?" James asked. "What happened to you?"

"Loss, I suppose."

"We've all lost."

Abe looked up and was no longer the boy James knew. The madness or the despair or the anger or the hate or all of them filled his eyes once more.

"If you don't want to see them, fine. Then you'll die a failed martyr with no followers."

"Is that what you think this is about?"

"Everyone wants to be a hero," Abe said.

"No, they don't," James said. He didn't, not anymore. "Not everyone. Just you." The rage in Abe's eyes seethed and spread. The pupils dilated and his cheeks flushed. The photo stayed on the floor. Abe reached into his pocket, pulled out a knife, and plunged it into James's chest. James should have screamed. He should have fought. He gasped for air, reached his arms out to Abe and instead of pushing, pulled him closer.

He tried to form a word, any word, any sound

other than the graveled gasps that escaped his throat. Abe pushed the knife deeper. The rage turned to tears. He looked more remorseful than invigorated. His lips quivered, embedded with crust and the stringy white saliva that formed when a person was filled with thirst. It was then James realized the sorrowful look on Abe's face, a look Abe had held for so long James hardly realized it as anything less than Abe's resting expression. That face was overrun with sadness, for all the people Abe could never save, like his parents, and all the ones he never knew he could, like James, like himself.

The pain was sharp but separate from James, almost as though it happened to someone else. The sky filled with birdcalls. James listened to the peaceful twitter. His gasps subsided. Abe helped James's body list to the ground. The snow didn't feel cold anymore.

The sunlight peaked over the trees. The last thing James saw: Abe's body walking away. He had stepped on the photo of them, leaving drops of James's blood to freeze over the glossy smiles of their past.

TASTE OF CRIMSON

ABE

THE AIR WAS WARM AND QUIET. ABE COULDN'T REMEMBER the last time he felt a day like this. That was the problem with good days, good times, laughs, and simple pleasures that once upon a time came too often. It was hard to remember specifics when those days were over. The memories of the beach in the sun faded. The scent of tacos and fresh tortillas disappeared a long time ago. Those memories had lasted longer than most. He couldn't remember the last sunny day or the last piece of chocolate or the last colorful flower he saw, or the last time he walked into a room that didn't smell like funk and shit. The sky held a pale leaden color. The sun shined bright. And Abe walked away, his back to his best friend.

James's eyes stared into the dome. Water dripped onto his face. Abe expected lifelessness, shame, terror, or pain smeared across James's face. But James smiled instead. When he had fallen to the floor Abe heard the small gasp, saw the smile, and started to cry. He finally understood why James didn't take the deal and didn't try to save himself. Maybe it was easier to stick to your convictions when you knew you would die soon either way. James had accepted it, or some part of it, like all the other times in their lives when all they could do was look at the lapse in their existence—their missing parents, their shitty home—and accept it.

Terror wrapped around Abe. It mixed pins and needles, cold and hot, pricked at his eyelids, pounded his stomach, and rose from his phantom finger. Terror was a word he didn't use often. He took excitement from fear. He relished his heart-beat. He reveled in the dark. He had loved fear.

Except terror was different. Terror was something he couldn't face. Terror was something he couldn't think of as excitement because it was something he couldn't confront. Bullies and weather, the ocean and wild dogs, lost parents and loneliness—those were fears he had taken on and shaken off. When the water dripped down onto James's face, Abe saw the smile and the warm look in James's eyes. Then he saw himself. He knew he couldn't escape. And that was when the terror set in. He made his way through the growing gray light filtering through the forest. The snow crisped under his feet. The trees encompassed him with frozen branches and a canopy made of icy leaves.

He and James had picked at the ice in San Diego to create a pathway for the cruise ship. James had fallen in; Abe hadn't. Tic-Tac dove in after James, Abe hadn't. Abe had been close and done nothing. It had been another moment of terror, watching his best friend slip beneath the ice. Abe never moved. This moment felt the same.

He looked around the trees and saw the lifeless landscape. He didn't want to deal with anyone.

When he had found Elise, blood had puddled on the floor and stained the sheets. He held her limp body in his arms and shook her. It felt natural to shake her at the time. He thought that at any minute she would come back to life, like when he slept and someone tapped his cheeks or tickled his feet and he sprung awake—Elise had needed to be shaken awake. Except she never woke up. James would never wake up either. In the company of the forest, Abe heard whispered screams sweep across the island. He swore they came from the cave. He kept walking and didn't stop until he reached the settlement, ready for the war to come.

SHAPELESS DISBELIEF

CHARLOTTE

THE DOGS WOKE CHARLOTTE UP WITH THEIR DEPRESSED whimpers. They nudged at her body and licked her face. She hadn't noticed when James left. She had wrapped her arms around herself in the night. She pushed Lee and Gray away. Diego and Sand curled around Autry. When was the last time Charlotte slept that well? *Food can do wonders*, she thought. The dogs pressed her again. They whined in fragile, high-pitched voices.

"You're already hungry?" she asked. "It was a feast last night."

They stepped toward the door and back near her again. They whimpered and growled.

"What's wrong with you two?" she asked.

"Shut those dogs up or I will," Tic-Tac said.

They nudged Charlotte again and stepped toward the cave's mouth. Whatever was wrong with them was at the door. She rubbed the food coma from her eyes and looked around the space. The usual bodies littered the ground. She expected to find Shia near the fire but he wasn't there. The dogs cried louder. A bad feeling crept into her mouth and tasted like bile. She ran through the cave looking for Shia's body, for his face, but didn't find him.

She nudged Tic-Tac awake. "Shia's gone," she said.

"So what?" he grumbled with his eyes still closed.

"The dogs are going nuts and Shia's gone."

"Can't this wait?"

"What if Abe's outside with a bunch of people waiting for us?"

"Then at least we'll be well rested."

"Really!"

"What if the dogs just want more fish?"

"What's happening?" Sarah asked.

"Forget it," Charlotte said.

"The dogs are hungry," Tic-Tac said.

Charlotte moved to the opening. Every deliberate step took her closer to the danger she assumed waited for her. She expected Abe with a bow and arrow aimed at her head, with an army of people behind him. The dogs urged her closer. Their whimpers turned to howls.

"Shut up!" Tic-Tac yelled.

The dogs and Charlotte moved closer until she reached the opening and saw no one at the tree line. The army wasn't there. The foothill was empty. Then she saw a photo with blood splatter on it. James's body lay nearby with blood frozen to his chest and a pained smile stuck to his lips. It couldn't have been James. She had held him last night. He had held her last night. They had held each other last night. They had kept each other warm. She ran to the body that couldn't have been James and held his head in her hands. She rubbed his cheeks and shook him. She slapped at his face. Finally, when he didn't wake up, she screamed. Sarah came out first, followed by Tic-Tac. They stopped and stared at Charlotte and the body.

He had been alive hours earlier, Charlotte thought. He had been alive and they had slept side-by-side curled up against each other. Tic-Tac sat next to Charlotte and wrapped his arm around her. She tried to shrug him away. She didn't want anyone to touch her. Tic-Tac held on tight and stared down at James's body. Sarah stood over them and rested her hand on Charlotte's shoulder.

"We need to get out of here," Charlotte said.

"I know," Tic-Tac said. They didn't have time to point fingers. The blame game could come later when they were safe elsewhere but right now they had to leave the cave behind before Abe decided to come back. "Help me up," he said.

The outliers came out of the cave little by little. Charlotte tried to wipe the blood off of James's coat. People's faces filled with worry. They needed to uproot again. At some point they had become nomads on an island with only one inhabitable space.

Time passed in immeasurable increments where seconds felt like an eternity. At some point, Tic-Tac had taken his arm away and turned to the formed crowd. "I know it's hard and we've asked a lot of you but we have to move one more time."

"Where?" Phil asked.

"We haven't even had a chance to scout," Cheryl said. "This was the last hideout on the island."

"We don't know that," Sarah said. "We just assumed that." Diego and Sand were calm, standing by Autry. Gray and Lee nudged Charlotte's arms. They pressed their wet noses to her exposed neck. They looked in the direction of any speaking voice. Their heads shifted back and forth following the sounds. "There will be another place for us, we just need to find it."

"Would you all rather stay here?" Charlotte

asked. She didn't look away from James. No one spoke. She couldn't stay in this place, not anymore.

"But what if—" Cheryl said.

"If what?" Charlotte asked. She wanted to run away from the cave and leave behind the shapeless disbelief. She wanted to scream at Tic-Tac and wake James up from the dead so she could kill him all over again for not believing that Shia would give them all away. The sadness and disbelief turned to anger and the anger would subside. For the first time in her life she wanted to kill somebody.

"We've done it before," Tic-Tac said. "This time we don't have dogs to worry about."

Gray and Lee, Diego and Sand barked. "Wild dogs," Tic-Tac said. "We don't have wild dogs to worry about."

Some people grumbled while others stayed silent. Tic-Tac turned to Charlotte and whispered, "I'm going to kill him. You and Sarah gather everyone and everything, and I'm going to kill him."

Tic-Tac started to walk down the hillside. The

dogs barked and whimpered. The crowd watched him fade into the trees. "Let's get ready to move," Sarah said. Charlotte agreed with Sarah but she didn't believe Tic-Tac. He may have wanted to kill Abe, but she would get to him first.

EYES OF INTENT

TIC-TAC

THE COLOR OF THE FOREST WAS BLEACHED WHITE MIXED with pure white. The army from the settlement stood out from the buildings made of ice, draped in snow leaves that dangled in the air, stuck to branches and outlining the trees that covered the sky.

The outliers had caught up to Tic-Tac on the walk through the woods.

"I told you to pack up and go," he said.

"We did," Sarah said. "We went—and we followed you." The rest of the outliers followed behind them. He saw Charlotte linger in the middle next to

Autry. Her face was resigned. Did she even register what had happened, what was about to happen?

Abe walked out from behind the tree, before the building in the distance. Sarah clung closer to Tic-Tac. He had stepped forward before Abe said a word. A crowd of people stood with arrows pointed at the outliers. The cold air struck Tic-Tac's face and visible smoke rose out of their volcanic crater where their abandoned home was. If they had ever had anything to lose, they didn't anymore. Tic-Tac stood tall and wanted to rush Abe. He was ready to take on the rest of the settlement and end this once and for all, then maybe he could return to his old room and take a hot bath.

More terror crept through his mind, stuck between Sarah's stop and the image of a hot bath, where he could even feel the boiling water wrap around his skin, almost too hot, singeing his hair and turning parts of his body a blotchy red.

"It's time for you to come home," Abe said.

"We should take them," Tic-Tac said. "All of them."

"Then what?" Sarah asked. "What happens next? Aren't you tired of fighting?"

"I'm tired of running."

The boys behind Abe steadied their aim. The army Charlotte had imagined that morning had come to life.

"He just wanted to come home," Abe said. "You should know about wanting to go home. We've all been there."

Tic-Tac pushed Sarah's arm away. The steps came swiftly. The snow made no sound under his boots, under his weight. He still felt full, for once, not worried about the relentless aching hunger. They had found hope too many times and watched it crushed by none other than themselves. He didn't want to deal with it anymore. He couldn't deal with it anymore. First their parents: gone. Then the only home most of them knew overrun by scavengers and snow: gone. Then the society they created: gone.

Then the cruise ship they found shelter in: gone. Even the shitty cave they squatted in: gone. What more could they be given that could be taken away?

The walk turned into a run. His surroundings swept past him with clarity. Charlotte's face filled with guilt. Abe had that continual shit-eating grin that hadn't left since he kissed Elise goodbye at her funeral, his lips to his fingers to her lips—he couldn't even get himself to kiss Elise's lips on his own. Now his lips were smeared with that grin that made him look as crazy as they all thought he was. Sarah's voice puffed behind him with the beginnings of a scream or a sob. Gray and Lee sat near Autry and sprang into action alongside Tic-Tac, their hackles and tails raised and sharp. Sand and Diego skulked lazily to the back of the pack to keep out of the trouble.

Abe shifted his weight and turned toward Tic-Tac. The dogs flashed past Abe, into the crowd of the settlers who had clubs and axes, ready for battle. The outliers held what they had carried with them from the cave, which was less than what they had carried from the ship, and which was even less than what they had carried from the settlement in the first place. Before Tic-Tac reached Abe, Charlotte's voice cracked from the tree line. It stopped Tic-Tac dead cold. The army lowered their weapons. A palpable cloud of confusion settled over everyone. The dogs even stopped running. Tic-Tac's rage escaped him. Uncertainty and fear replaced it.

"Challenge," Charlotte had said. "I challenge Abe."

If Abe really wanted them all to come back together this wasn't the way to do it. Hatred had grown from fear and turned them all against one another, broken ice that couldn't be put back together. Everything expired in the rabid anger that wouldn't help any of them. Except even surrounded by the hate and the cries and the blood, filled with the knowledge that the more they fought, the weaker they became, Tic-Tac couldn't turn away from Charlotte. Her face contorted into a small smile.

ARROGANCE
OF RESTRAINT

ABE

ABE'S GRATITUDE FOR CHARLOTTE FELL SHORT OF HIS DESIRE to feel his own face smashed to a pulp, whether to experience how it felt or rid himself of the emptiness that relentlessly reminded him of where they all were, he wasn't sure. It didn't matter. The fight had started and Abe needed to stand up and end it. *Cut the head off the snake and the body dies.* If he took out Charlotte, the rest of the outliers would fall in line and return back to the settlement, return to the rules that would shape and protect them all, take away this swarm of madness and replace it with order, their order, his order, and no more blood would be shed. Too much had taken them away from the safety of where their lives should have been, and it started with the world before them. They shouldn't have to live according to the rules forced on them before their lifetimes. It had doomed them all. The outcry of unfairness and craze would end now.

They would all have to stand together soon, once the outliers gave up, and he would rather have them in good health and good shape to fit back into the settlement without harm or memory of the life outside. They needed to reshape themselves, pick the remnants of themselves from off the floor and realize that both sides had spilled blood for a cause, for reasons they believed in. They were more alike than different.

His body trembled, less from the cold and more from the anger ripping through his veins and bulging in his eyes. He came to the island to protect them and now lacked the power to keep them from killing one another. He looked to the trees, to the leaves, to the torn clothes.

"It didn't need to be like this," Abe said.

"How else could it have been?" Charlotte asked. She walked past Tic-Tac. Sarah stood by the tree line with the rest of the outliers.

"If we're all going to go out together anyway," Abe said.

When she reached Abe, in what felt like a blink of an eye, he pushed her to the floor, smeared ice over her face and then propped her up. He pressed the cold steel edge of the knife against her neck. The blade had remnants of his crusted blood. He wanted it to stay there as commemoration of his sacrifice to the settlement; Abe was willing to give up parts of himself for all of them.

"What are your last thoughts going to be of?" Abe asked. "James? Or how painful this will be? How about regret because you never should have challenged me. This isn't how people survive."

"They're your rules," Charlotte said. Tic-Tac yelled something with a harsh tone Abe couldn't understand. Anxiety poured out of the outliers and smelled like sugar.

"You made the challenge," Abe said. "It'll be over soon." He pulled Charlotte's hair and pressed the blade deeper into her neck. His knee dug into her back between her shoulder blades. If she could move she would have done it by now. Drool ran down the corners of her mouth. "You too afraid to swallow."

"Coward," she said.

"What was that?"

"This is done," Tic-Tac shouted. Abe tilted Charlotte's head back. He wanted to see what she saw, the treetops and the gunmetal sky. The tranquil silence of the forest surrounded them all now, undercut by the yells of the outliers to let Charlotte go. They sounded like angry birds pecking at the inside of his ears.

"I wanted to let you know how easy it would be for me to slide this across your throat," Abe said.

"Then it would be done." He loosened the pressure of the knife on her skin.

"It'll still be done," she said. She spit an excess of saliva to the ground. A sliver of blood remained where the blade had been. She didn't touch her neck. She almost fell flat on her face. She wrapped herself in her arms and Abe remembered what that felt like. How weak had he been the last time he needed that much comfort? When Elise died he thought he would never unwrap himself from his arms, the bed sheets, the warmth of his room. Now the outliers were the weak ones and he wanted to eradicate weakness all together.

Charlotte looked at Tic-Tac and Sarah. "I thought I was helping."

It took four boys to peel her away. She didn't kick or scream. She looked emotionless, like an iceberg floating away.

"I'm not running away," Charlotte said to Abe.

"This time," Abe said, "I'm just making sure."

"We'll do it," Tic-Tac said. The boys backed

away. Tic-Tac and Sarah each took one side of Charlotte. "This is for all of us."

The settlement and the outliers returned to the settlement. It should have been a happy moment but all the cheers of victory never came.

NEVER HAD
A CAGED BIRD
TIC-TAC

THE ROOM THAT USED TO BE THE COMMITTEE WAS EMPTY except for Tic-Tac and Sarah. The two of them had not seen any of the outliers since they were taken to the settlement. Tic-Tac didn't know what the room might have been used for since. It once stood as a meeting place for the community, a symbol of their survival, past, present, and future. The room felt the same, but in the ever-changing tide of their lives, "same" became a loaded word. For all Tic-Tac knew they could have used the room to slit people's throats and drain them of their blood, stringing up the bodies before they started to decay, and hanging them outside for everyone to see. Warning signs for betrayers and free thinkers. He hadn't noticed a body or any signs of punishment when they walked into the main square yesterday. That worried him more than it comforted him—if he had seen punishment, he'd at least know what to expect. Not knowing always made it worse.

Abe had led Tic-Tac, and Sarah followed with Charlotte. When they reached the cell house, two guards took Charlotte away. Another six guards separated Tic-Tac and Sarah from the pack, leading them one way and the rest of the outliers to another. They hadn't been treated poorly. They were fed and given blankets to sleep on, not that they needed blankets in the heat of the committee. Tic-Tac wanted to wrap himself up in the heat. He could never explain how comfortable he felt when the heat was so uncomfortable, but he hadn't been warm for so long that he would be happy overheating.

Sarah seemed to feel the same way. She had snuggled up to him the moment they entered the committee and he hadn't wanted to let go. They had spent too much time apart already, split between their nightmares, the settlement, the cruise ship, the forest, and the cave. They hadn't had a moment alone together since before she left for the ship. Before that, he had spent most of the time in his own head, torn away from reality, watching his own mind spin out of control. Then the Northern Lights, a premature reassurance of their existence, went away. It wasn't until she left that he realized how far he had spun away from where he needed to be. When she wrapped her arms around him in the uncomfortable comforts of the warm room, he felt at home. He had not felt that comfort since they'd first jumped into bed together on the cruise ship.

Dinner came the first night. Tic-Tac devoured his stew in one gulp that plastered uncontrollable joy over his face once more. He had been so hungry he hadn't noticed the voices of the guards at first.

"I know," a voice said. "I just want a banana, like a full one, or something. I, like, crave it."

"What are you lis—" Sarah said. Tic-Tac covered her mouth. When the guards went silent Sarah continued eating but Tic-Tac never told her why he cared to listen in the first place.

In the morning, breakfast came. Tic-Tac ate deer sausage and powdered eggs and reveled in the taste of fake eggs in a way he never thought he would. Then lunch came: another hearty helping of stew that tasted better than the night before. At night they ate spaghetti. Tic-Tac couldn't remember the last time he had noodles. The tomatoes were sweet and acidic but there wasn't much sauce. He dipped his fingers into whatever watery flavor he could find and sucked the sauce away. He had eaten four meals in a row and felt strong, alive, but a bit sick from too much food. His stomach told him to eat more and more, and when the food was gone he wasn't hungry yet craved more.

He sat by the door again.

"There's not even any sauce this time," the same guard from last night complained. Tic-Tac heard

the disappointment and anger in the guard's voice. This kid didn't know what it was like to go hungry, yet he complained about shitty spaghetti sauce. "Those assholes get more sauce than we do." *He can only be referring to us,* Tic-Tac thought.

"They're running out of food," he whispered to Sarah.

"No way," she said in disbelief. They just ate four full meals. The last thing he wanted or could imagine would be another lack of food, another point of starvation. He shushed Sarah again.

"Not completely," he said. "I think the greenhouse is dying, or at least not producing."

"What does that mean for us?"

"I've been listening to those two assholes complain about food. Every time they open their mouths, it's about what they don't have."

"If only they'd spent time in the cave." Sarah smiled.

"They only complained about things that grew

in the greenhouse. Either it's already dead or Abe's rationing because it's dying."

"Charlotte and Autry were the only two green-thumbs this place had. Seems they took those thumbs with them," Sarah said.

Small lights shined through the window and rotated on the floor. Tic-Tac looked out the window and saw the dancing colors of the Northern Lights. They had been absent from the sky long enough for Tic-Tac to think they had disappeared with the rest of the world. When the lights across the sky stopped dancing, Tic-Tac had believed time forgot them, the lights, him, Sarah, the settlement. He thought time was as tangible as the snow, and equally frozen. They all existed outside of the physics that once ruled them, when the earth revolved around the sun and seasons meant food and shelter and birth and death. The world stopped revolving and the settlement sat at the center of the motionless world, where time was a memory in the paradox of memories, which couldn't exist if time didn't exist, because how could they? That wasn't the point, Tic-Tac told himself. When the light returned, he realized he was wrong. Time hadn't forgotten them. At times like these, he didn't mind being wrong.

The door opened and two guards came in wielding bows. Abe followed them in. The boys looked too young to be his personal guards and must have been the two standing outside the door. Tic-Tac wondered how much of Fornland they could remember, how much of their lives they remembered before this place. How much of his own life could he remember before this place? The guards probably didn't remember much if they were bitching about bananas and spaghetti sauce.

"Guys," Abe said to the boys. "We don't need that. Right?" He turned to Tic-Tac who stepped toward Sarah near the far wall. Abe told the guards to go.

"You boys want some spaghetti sauce?" Tic-Tac asked. "I've got a little more." They hesitated before walking out. Abe tried to hide his confusion and closed the door behind them.

"Where is everyone else?" Sarah asked.

Abe drew a line with his foot across the floor. "Everyone behind this line is safe," Abe said. "What bad thing could possibly happen?"

"I think we need to talk," Tic-Tac said. He had spent more time with Abe inside the settlement walls than anyone. Even as Abe's mind slipped further away from what he once had been, Abe always calculated his steps. He wouldn't have come to them without a reason. If Tic-Tac was right, they knew the reason, but they didn't know the plan.

"That's the first reasonable thing I've heard come out of this room in a long time," Abe said.

"Then talk," Tic-Tac said. "You've already got something on your mind, I'm sure."

"It's not a hard conversation," Abe said.

The decision of whether to live or die was more than just about the desire to live, but about the quality of life that would come after. What would

Tic-Tac be giving up if he renounced his past actions to survive? Every action they made until now was to survive another day; how would this one be any different?

"I'd rather die," Sarah said.

"Sounds like you've already made your choice," Abe said.

"No one's decided anything," Tic-Tac said. "Let's all come down. You promise everyone else is already settled in?"

Abe nodded.

"Then let me take Charlotte's place," Tic-Tac said.

"Don't—" Sarah said.

"That's not how this works," Abe said.

"You change the fucking rules when you feel like it," Tic-Tac said. "No one would question it."

"I would," Abe said. "She made her choice."

"What about our choices?" Tic-Tac asked.

"Who said you all get a choice? I'm sure this isn't exactly what you had in mind but it can't be far off from what you figured *would* happen. They all followed you out there. And they'll keep following you too. I'd rather make sure they follow you back across this line and stay there."

If they kept themselves separate from Abe maybe they had a chance of collecting the outliers and taking over. The longer Tic-Tac stayed in the room, the more food they fed him, the less he wanted to venture back out into the deep freeze. But if they hadn't been able to take over before, why would they be able to do it now? The light continued to dance through the window near the line at Abe's feet. Tic-Tac wanted to spit on it rather than cross it, but sometimes comfort could be overwhelming.

"There's a group of young kids out there who believed in you all. They might find it hard to believe in you when you're dead. Or worse—when they're dead."

"You wouldn't?" Sarah asked.

"You're lucky I'm even giving you this option."

Tic-Tac grabbed Sarah's shoulders. Sarah stood stunned, whether with anger, fear, or shock, Tic-Tac couldn't tell. It didn't matter what her motives were, this is where it led them. They had to give themselves up as liars or failures to the kids who had followed them into the cold and almost starved to death. But with full pantries and warm rooms, would anyone care one way or the other? Unless they could renegotiate the deal.

"I think your greenhouse wants a different deal," Tic-Tac said.

"What are you—" Abe stopped himself. Composure had always been important at Fornland. It didn't matter how you felt but how you acted. You didn't cry, even if you wanted to, and you didn't get mad, even if you were ready to explode. Abe had always been good at not betraying himself, until now.

"From what I gather it looks like you've been having trouble with the farm."

"And you're delusional."

Tic-Tac could feel the momentum swing to them. The heat felt embracing. Sweat dribbled down his back and he loved every second of it. Abe's face contorted as it tried to hide his anger. *How could they have known*, he seemed to think.

Because we listen, Tic-Tac thought, *something you haven't done in years*.

"What are you going to do if the plants die, Abe? We at least know what it's like out there without supplies. Most of those kids don't."

"That's why you would do what you can to protect them," Abe said. "You don't want to go back out there."

"You don't want us to go. Death doesn't really appeal to me," Tic-Tac said. "You?" he asked Sarah. Her smile was bright and captivating. Tic-Tac had missed that smile.

"I don't believe death is my cup of tea," Sarah said.

Abe cringed with the intensity of a cat dropped in a bucket of frigid water. His anger turned to laughter and the laughter made Tic-Tac want to puke.

"What's so funny?" Tic-Tac asked.

"You," Abe said. "You think you can come here and back me into a corner. You know the saying; never underestimate a cornered animal." A sharp tingle shot up Tic-Tac's spine. In tic-tac-toe he had always seen an end game where each spot could bring him closer to a win if he caught his opponent off guard. He didn't expect to be the one trapped.

"You're right," Abe said. "I didn't expect you to find out about the greenhouse. But let's be honest. You've got no legs to stand on. Charlotte is in the dome tomorrow. You take her place and she works the greenhouse. You plead for mercy and she works the greenhouse. She fights, I kill her, and then force Autry to work the greenhouse. We may have *had* a problem, but once Charlotte challenged me, all our problems disappeared."

"You really are a twisted son of a bitch," Tic-Tac said.

"Those are the ones that survive," Abe said. He didn't wait for a response. He turned around and closed the door behind him.

A brief silence settled over the room. Tic-Tac hadn't thought about failure, didn't even think it was an option. He should have pounced Abe in the woods even after Charlotte made the challenge. Tic-Tac's anger turned inwards, attaching itself to what he thought was weakness and stupidity.

"Save themselves," Sarah said. "That's all anyone does now."

"You don't have to tell me," Tic-Tac said. "I have always—"

"No, you *had* always. Then we came here and that part of you died, just a little at first, but the longer we were here the more it shriveled. I don't blame you, but I'm telling you it did." Sarah kissed Tic-Tac on the cheek, pressed her back to his chest, and wrapped his arms around her. "You have always made me feel safe," she said. "Others want to feel the same."

The anger continued to rattle around his insides, a volcano in his stomach, a geyser in his mind.

But "safe" was a word he had almost forgotten about. Living was more than surviving. They should value one over the other.

REDUNDANTLY NUMB

CHARLOTTE

CHARLOTTE SPAT ON THE WALL. THE SLITHERING WETNESS streaked down the creases of the wood. She rubbed the edges of her palms. They were red and raw. She thought of all the people who had gone through life without feeling sensation. Could she do that? Was it too late to try? What would it take for her to drift through this place without any feeling at all, where if someone touched her hand, she wouldn't even notice? If someone slapped her in the face, she would sleep through it. If someone broke her nose, she wouldn't wake up. She searched for that feeling, hoped for that feeling, so when the pain of starving and freezing became too much, she wouldn't have even noticed.

Now she sat in a room with a full stomach and heat, but she still wished she felt nothing. The more she felt, the harder it was to breathe. A rock sat on her lungs and pressed down. She rubbed her fingers over her palms and tried to breathe slowly—in and out. The directions weren't hard, but the application was. *In and out, breathe, slow breaths.* But the more she tried, the shallower her breaths came. Her wrists hurt. Her hands hurt. Her heart hurt. Her lungs hurt. She wanted to find a way to stop feeling anything at all. It would be easier.

"We wouldn't have made it," she said. "We were hanging on by our skin and we had nothing left."

"We had each other," James's voice responded.

"How would that be enough? Was I supposed to eat you when you died? Would that have helped us more than if you were around?"

"I would have thought of something." His voice resounded in her head, bouncing off the walls of the cell, inescapable, as if she wanted to escape his voice at all. She wanted to embrace him, but he was never really there.

"But you hadn't. How long were we supposed to wait?" Charlotte asked.

"I could have saved us!"

She wanted to believe that he could have, that James still had it in him to be a hero, the hero that they wanted, that they needed—that he needed himself to become. He didn't want to be the helpless, hapless person he saw himself to be, who needed saving at every turn, from the water, from the Icedome, from an old fight, from smoke, from starvation. He never was that person, Charlotte had told him.

"I usually believe you," she said, "but not this time." She reached for the space where she wished James to be. In the moment of turmoil, her hand would have been soft through the glove, her touch would have been empathetic and understanding, ready to make it all better just because she reached for him, was with him. Except within the screams of battle, when the snow started to look more like a slaughterhouse floor than a mountain resort, and every breath pierced the air with another slap, punch, kick, stab, or bite, he stepped away from her. She couldn't make this right.

"I just wanted to go home," she said.

"We all did," he said.

She wanted out of this place. Maybe someone would come with her. James would have come with her. She couldn't take James, not anymore. Soon she would be in the Icedome fighting for her life. Her death would come slow, painful, and prolonged. The snow could numb the pain, maybe, making sure whatever part of her hurt was buried in ice would hurt less.

"You get any sleep?" Sarah asked. Charlotte's eyes were closed. Sarah sat next to the cage. She grunted. "Stiff legs."

"I slept a little."

"Let me see your hands."

Charlotte gave Sarah her hands through the cage. Sarah's hands were callused but warm. Charlotte's felt dry and cracked. If she blew on them they might turn to dust and blow away.

"I thought maybe—" Charlotte said.

"You can't keep hounding yourself over this," Sarah said. "It would have ended up this way one way or another."

"You don't know that," Charlotte said.

"Yes, I do. That's how it's always been. We wouldn't have made it out there any longer. You saw an opening and tried. That's more than most others can say."

Tic-Tac leaned against the far wall. His eyes were red with sleep. He looked caught somewhere between awake and uncomfortable. An invisible wall stood around him, not letting anyone close—just him, his red eyes, and his body.

"I wonder how it could've played out," Sarah said.

"All we have is what did and didn't happen,"

Tic-Tac said. "We aren't on some sandy beach drinking margaritas and getting a tan. We ended up here, warm for once but still surrounded by fucking snow."

"I didn't—" Charlotte tried to say.

"Charlotte, it doesn't matter what you did or didn't mean to do. This isn't a gift. It's not the thought that counts anymore. You're going into that dome."

Empty, that was how it all felt now. She was empty of caring, empty of wanting, empty of hope. Sarah let go of Charlotte's hands. Charlotte wished Sarah had held on for longer. She found consolation in Sarah's touch, someone's touch. She could run anywhere on the island, but what good would it do her? She couldn't keep herself from pain. She couldn't keep herself from starvation. "We want to make sure you're the one that comes out," Sarah said.

"There might be another way," Charlotte said.

"Now you're just delusional," Tic-Tac said.

"Stop it," Sarah said. "Sometimes you can be an asshole."

"You can't always be the bearer of good news, especially when there isn't any."

"He's right," Charlotte said.

"Does that mean you have a plan?" Tic-Tac asked.

"Yes," Charlotte said.

"Go on," Sarah said.

"We give up," Charlotte said. "He who fights and runs away . . ."

"Doesn't have the courage to fight another day," Tic-Tac said.

"But at least has the chance to," Charlotte said. She wrapped her hands in the cushions of her sleeves. "You don't have to like it. You don't have to follow it. But I'm going to survive this and make it better, like this all never happened."

"That's great," Tic-Tac said. "Except it has happened. And I won't forget that."

He turned away from Charlotte and walked to the

door. Charlotte watched Sarah's eyes search her up and down. She wondered what Sarah was looking for, or if she found it. Charlotte had nothing to hide and nowhere to hide it. In the quiet room that suddenly felt too hot and too enclosed, Sarah walked over to Tic-Tac, took his hand, and kissed his palm. The simple gesture brought back the giant stone that compressed Charlotte's heart. No matter how many times she tried to tell herself that she couldn't have saved James, she couldn't help but break, little by little, under the circling realization that James was gone.

Tic-Tac left but Sarah stayed behind.

"He's worried about you," Sarah said.

"He shouldn't be."

"Cut the shit, Charlotte. No one else is here." Before Charlotte could respond, Sarah ignored the look on Charlotte's face and continued. "You spent enough time in this place to know what we have, and it's not sitting in some stupid greenhouse. Of course, Tic-Tac was ready to take Abe. He was about to. Then you opened your mouth. Now you could die and Tic-Tac's pissed he couldn't save you. What did you expect?"

"Peace, maybe? Or a little bit of fucking gratitude," Charlotte said. "This will be over one way or another by the end of today."

"What do you think Abe will do with us if you lose? We'll suddenly be safe?"

"It'll—"

"No, Charlotte. This is about you and retribution. It'll be over, sure, but at what cost?"

"Whatever it takes," Charlotte said.

"Spoken like a true asshole." Sarah went to walk out the door but paused. Charlotte didn't notice the crinkle in Sarah's coat pocket. "I found this. You look like you need it more than I hoped you would." She slid the photo of Abe, Elise, and James through the bars. "There are still people who care about you."

When Sarah left, the quiet warmth of the room turned toxic. James's face was marred with thawed blood splatter that started to streak. It turned his smile into a sneer.

FAMILIAR PLACES

CHARLOTTE

IN THE MORNING LIGHT TWO BOYS GRABBED CHARLOTTE AND
she knew what would come next. This time she
wouldn't escort James in his last minutes of somber
light. This time she wouldn't run away into the
trees and hide in a room or in the crowd or a distant
memory. The guards had come in and told her to
strip.

"Turn around," she said.

They did.

"No peeking," she said. She put on the white
shroud that fighters wore when they fought in the
dome. The guards took her clothes. They took her

shoes. They opened the bars and let her walk free for a minute. She braced herself for the cold.

"How is it out there?" she asked. The fear didn't hit her. She didn't feel sadness toward Sarah, but her insides raged with resentment toward Abe. She wrapped her hands around her arms in anticipation of the chill.

"The same," one of the guards said. He looked familiar. Charlotte recognized the boy's face but the name escaped her. He had childish brown eyes and a weak chin. He looked more indifferent than proud.

"I knew you," she said. She had been gone for so long that people had grown and she hadn't realized it. Faces once filled with childish chub now looked firm and strong, bodies bulky, eyes filled with more than mischief.

"You knew us both," the other guard said. His eyes were bright and blue like the ice. His nose was flat. They both were young but tall. He wore the same look of indifference.

"I'm sure I did," Charlotte said. "At some point in time."

"I never wanted you to leave," the first guard said.

"Me neither," the second guard said.

"I had never planned on leaving until it happened," she said. "That's usually how it works."

The first guard said, "I thought it would get better." The second guard nodded.

"It doesn't," she said. "It just doesn't." She looked away.

They opened the door and Charlotte cringed. She stepped through the frame. She held tight to her skin and looked around at the empty village. The guards closed the door behind her and grabbed her arms. Their gloves were rough. They irritated her biceps. She unlatched her tight grip and watched her skin shift from lifeless to rosy. She took a step off of the porch and pressed her bare feet onto the ice, except she didn't feel the cold. The ice wasn't warm, but it didn't make her freeze. She didn't feel the need to cover herself with her arms. The air didn't burn with bitter winter. The sunlight reflected off of the snow and she squinted her eyes.

The sunlight reflected off of the snow. In the sky the sun shined bright. The gray had disappeared. The sky was an open blue, an empty open blue that seemed to stretch endlessly. Charlotte smiled and kept walking.

"You guys can let go," she said. "I'm not going anywhere."

They nodded to her and let go of her arm. Each continued to stare ahead with their indifferent eyes. The dome loomed over Charlotte's head as each step carried her closer. The chants echoed in the empty blue sky. "One winner! One life!" The guards didn't join the cry. The chant seemed weaker than Charlotte remembered. The last time James had made this walk, the sound resounded through the settlement in a way that shook the earth and felt like the volcano had erupted and would soon shatter the greenhouse glass. The echoes carried the line but without the fervor and strength it once had.

"One winner, one life?" Charlotte looked at the guards. They shook their heads.

"It hasn't worked so far," the first guard said. The second nodded in ascent.

She broke a smile. "You got that right."

When they came to the dome's gates, Charlotte felt the lackluster call continue. The doors opened and she felt the guards watch her as she stepped into the dome.

"Good luck," one whispered. Charlotte wasn't sure which one. The words sunk beneath the crowd. The last time James had entered the dome, she had hid like a coward in the greenhouse, unable to watch the probable outcome that he would lose. The icy bars that created the arena were firm and blue. The crowd had pounded their fists and stomped their feet. They screamed and cursed. They had wanted blood. She imagined Geoff's eyes lusting for blood. James had survived in this place of blood and worship. Now she made the same walk in the same place, but it didn't mean it was all the same.

The dome was slick and smooth. The giant initials Abe had once carved into the surface were gone. Abe stood on the far side of the arena and looked more sullen than bloodthirsty. Charlotte stopped and so did the chant. It didn't linger or echo. There were no remnants of the words. They simply disappeared as if they had never existed. *How perfect it would be to never have existed at all,* Charlotte thought. What would the world look like if she had left it long ago, instead of her parents, instead of Elise, instead of James? Would Abe be the benevolent leader they all thought he could be? Would they have made it to the island at all?

One simple choice would ripple through eternity. What choices had she made? Charlotte imagined Abe sitting near the water with a drink in his hand, an umbrella sticking out of the glass. Elise sat next to him holding his hand. They sat in lawn chairs on the snowy shore but it didn't look cold. James came out of the ocean and slicked the water back out of his hair. They all looked happy, like the photo Charlotte had left in the cell, full of old smiles and new blood. That wasn't their life and no matter how much Charlotte thought about what life could have been, it didn't change the fact that life was bitter, unfair, and here. Except it wasn't as cold as she remembered.

"You can still change your mind," Abe said. The crowd was silent. A short breeze made more noise than the collected breaths of the settlement.

"No," she said. "I can't." Calm had taken over. Her heart beat evenly. Her mouth filled with the thick mixture of mucus and spit, the hard saliva of thirst. When she looked at Abe, she saw the embodiment of anger. Her body shook and her mind emptied, replacing every thought with a single purpose, not a purpose but a desire: to kill him. She spit and the slime splattered on the floor where Abe and Elise's initials had once been. The sunlight beamed down onto the center of the dome. She let the warmth linger on her skin. The crowd loomed over the bars, their faces enduring, the bloodlust missing. She found Sarah. Her eyes were as clear as the sky, focused on Charlotte. The white tips of Charlotte's hair brushed past her breasts and dangled near her belly button. She though she saw James's face in the crowd, lingering with same intent and curious eyes, anxious about what would happen next.

Abe raised his hand. "One winner! One life!" he said. No one responded. The fight had begun.

ONE WINNER

CHARLOTTE

THE EDGES OF THE DOME WERE CRISP AND BRIGHT AND BLUE. Charlotte pushed the quiet crowd aside. She wrapped her fingers in her fist and tried to pinch her nails into her skin. *Make sure I'm not dreaming,* she thought. She was ready to wake up in her own bed, drenched in sweat with a new nightmare having taken over the familiar dark walls of her parents' car crash. The tiny piercing of her nails into her palms told her this wasn't a dream. She and Abe circled each other. They didn't dance. They walked. They stepped around each other. Abe looked despaired. They edged closer and closer, each step taking one of them closer to death—one winner, one life.

The light used to guide her home. She thought that at least. She thought the sun would be a beacon to bigger and better things. When the sun disappeared, she hadn't noticed it at first. The longer the sun stayed stuck behind the clouds the more she realized the emptiness of the sky, the light, herself, the adventure that turned out to be more than she bargained for. The light had died. Except now it came back and spread over the snow, the blinding snow. *Was it a joke?* She didn't feel like it had been replaced. The hope that she would be guided to something bigger and better had drowned somewhere in the frozen sea. It never came back, even in the blanket of sunlight that now came from nowhere, with no warning.

"It won't help," she said.

"It isn't supposed to," Abe said. Then he lunged. The crowd gasped. Charlotte looked up at Abe. He slammed his fist into her cheek. She fell to the floor.

"This is gonna be a short one," Phil said dismally.

"You shut the fuck up or I will eat you alive," Sarah said.

Charlotte didn't want to let the tears out. Her mother once told her that people only had a certain amount of tears in their lifetime. "Don't waste them all at once," her mom had said.

Charlotte tried not to waste them when her parents died. But over the last few days, she thought she let them all out. She wanted to let them all out. She didn't want to hold onto her tears any longer. Maybe her mom was wrong, another disappointment in a lifetime of disappointments. Abe's fists felt harder. They felt permanently molded to her cheek.

Charlotte and Abe fought in the center of the dome. Abe straddled Charlotte and punched and punched and punched and punched. The air was punctuated with the sounds of Abe's fist to her bones. The crowd was silent. The visible wisps of air with every person's breath were gone. Charlotte couldn't breathe. She made herself watch Abe's fists coming down. She thought of James and wanted punishment. She couldn't get to him in time, to protect him like she said she would.

"Stop it!" Sarah screamed.

Tic-Tac grabbed Sarah and pulled her away from the bars.

Abe's breath was hot on Charlotte's skin. It smelled like rotting teeth. She hated it. She hated him. She hated everyone. She elbowed him. Nothing happened. She twisted and shook her head. Abe didn't move. Another fist broke bone, the awful crunch, sickening. Another punch. Another punch.

"Please," she whispered.

"You don't," Abe said. His voice was soft. She heard pain in his tone. It dripped with sorrow like a drying puddle. Everyone was quiet. The air was still. A whimper filtered through the bars of the dome. The whimper came and went with a perfect escape. It lifted into the sky, somehow pathetic and beautiful. Her eyes were bloodshot. Pain was such a harrowed beast it could contort a person's face to something you could have never imagined. She had memorized every freckle and dimple on James's face. She remembered how they shifted and moved after his fall through the ice, after his fight with Geoff. The dimples made a permanent home on his face, less from a smile and more from the scars. Would that be her face now, reshaped by Abe's fists?

She had expected Abe's last hit but the force surprised her. She heard her cheek crack before she felt it. Her jaw slipped sideways. She didn't have a chance to cover up. Black spots smothered her vision. Ringing filled the air. The sun disappeared into darkness. The dome went silent. It couldn't have been silent. The dome was never silent. Sanguine flooded the air. She felt the blood filling her mouth more than Abe's fists. The energy drained from her body. She relished the cold ice against her back. She wanted to roll over and press her cheek to the ground and let the blood spill out of her body. She tried to roll over. She couldn't roll over. Abe pinned Charlotte's shoulders to the floor. One punch. Another punch. She could see for a second. Then her eyes were drenched in blood and the sun disappeared behind the crimson. Another punch. Loud barks and growls penetrated the silence. Snarls wrapped around the dome. Abe let up his grip enough for Charlotte to escape.

She threw her open palm into Abe's nose. Blood splattered out. His hands tried to cover the break. Charlotte pulled Abe close in her arms and sunk her teeth into the soft cartilage of his ear. Abe screamed. She didn't care. She clamped down until the cartilage crunched, broke. Thick liquid filled her mouth. She tore her teeth away and ripped Abe's ear with it. Charlotte spit the cartilage to the floor with the rest of the sprawling shit. The dome had become a slaughterhouse, like when Teagan butchered a deer, only this time the deer fought back.

Charlotte shoved Abe away. He rolled on the floor in pain. She kicked him in the stomach and felt the anger run through her leg. It was the same feeling as the endless hunger she felt in the cave. She looked down at him and saw a pathetic, bloody mess.

"Guess it's a fight," Abe said. His voice reverberated, caught in a blood bubble.

Charlotte wiped the blood from her eyes and it smeared across her skin. She tried again. The puddle on the floor expanded into a lake and Charlotte didn't know how much of it had come from her wounds or from Abe's.

"Something . . . " she could barely speak. She couldn't gather enough air no matter how hard she tried. "To . . . remember me . . . by."

Abe pressed his hand to his head. Pressing flesh to blood didn't stop the bleeding. Abe wouldn't miss his ear; he never listened anyway.

Then the dome faded away. The crowd disappeared. Abe no longer stood at the edge of the circle screaming. Charlotte saw it but couldn't believe it. It could've been the blood in her eyes. She had been hit over and over again. She saw it. A drop of water fell from the dome. When she thought she had made it up another drop fell. It sunk into the puddle of blood and splashed. She looked up at the bars. Another drop fell. Another drop. Another drop. The bars were melting. The dome would melt. The ice would melt. She smiled with relief.

CHARLOTTE

Charlotte had forgotten about the silence of pain. She had blocked out the quiet scream she couldn't control when her parents died. It returned now. Her throat was thick and bulging. She could choke on her own silence. Her tongue flared. Her skin crawled. No matter how much she tried to make a sound, nothing came out, not a scream, a cry, or a breath. Her bones felt brittle and her muscles went slack.

Abe continued to kneel, his hands pressed to his

ear, blood pouring from his face, staining his body and the ground. The dome dripped. The more she stared at Abe, the more paralyzed she became. His eyes opened and beamed at her. She wanted to end it, to end him. Seconds earlier she was ready to. Then she saw the ice melting. The anger stayed but the rage subsided.

"Do it," Abe said. Charlotte saw another drop fall. "You have to. You want to. I see it. I know that look. Get it over with."

Charlotte drove her knee into his face. She stood over him with her fists balled ready to pummel Abe into death, a place where she could forget him.

"Do it!" he screamed. The echo made the dogs yelp. "You have to."

Charlotte shook her head. She couldn't. Every inch of her wanted to, from her toes to her fingers, but she couldn't. She didn't want to be any more like Abe than she already felt, and that scared the shit out of her.

"Kill me!" he said with a softer voice, a sound

she couldn't imagine from Abe, one that drifted only between the two of them. "Please." She didn't. She couldn't. Abe collapsed on the floor, defeated. The crowd stayed silent. The dogs stayed quiet. Charlotte looked up. Guards came into the dome. She hesitated. Her face continued to bleed. The guards scooped up Abe.

"We can handle this," the first guard said.

"No," she said. "Put him in the cage until he heals, then he'll be back with the rest of us. One winner, one life is done."

The guards took Abe away, leaving behind the weak ruffle of his body dragging in the snow.

NO ROOM
FOR BANDAGES

SARAH

THE INFIRMARY STRETCHED OUT IN AN ENDLESS ROW OF BEDS, filled with a chill Sarah knew wasn't actually there. Charlotte lay on the bed, motionless. The guards had brought her in after the dome. First they had carried Abe to the cell.

"He can be treated there," Charlotte said. Then she swayed, rocked, and fell over, all energy or adrenaline washing away, Sarah imagined. The guards had rushed over to Charlotte, carried her away, and laid her down safely on a bed. Sarah followed them.

From outside the dome, Charlotte had looked pummeled, her face mimicking what Sarah could only imagine the inside of her body looked like, wearing a mask made of blood, bone, and muscle. Up close Charlotte's face was worse. Sarah swallowed a gasp when she entered the room, not that Charlotte would have noticed; she was passed out. Her face barely resembled the person she was before she entered the dome. Her jaw tilted to the right. Her cheekbone broke into puzzle pieces. Even the whites of her eyes had turned red, the blood capsules popped inside the cornea leaving a film of crimson. *Could she even see it?* Sarah wondered. Rudy rushed into the room. "How's she doing?" he asked.

"Where were you?" Sarah asked.

"The dome . . . "

"It's fine," Sarah said. "I don't care. But she looks like death on a stick."

Rudy took off his gloves and pressed his fingers to Charlotte's pulse. He held a small piece of glass over her nose to check her breathing; archaic but effective. "She's alive," Rudy said. "That's saying something. She took one hell of a beating."

"You should see the other guy," Sarah said.

"I will," Rudy said.

"He's alive too," Sarah said.

"You're joking," Rudy said.

"She couldn't do it."

"I know how she—I mean . . . I almost did, a week ago, when Abe came in here asking me to cut his finger off. I should have just let the thing fester, get infected, and kill him."

"He probably would have done it himself at that point," Sarah said.

Rudy gave an exhaled laugh, the absurdity of Abe cutting off his own finger made worse because it probably would have happened.

"I had the knife in my hand. Claire held him down. I could have done it. It would have saved James. It would have saved Charlotte from this."

"It wasn't you," Sarah said.

"But—"

"It wasn't you. No one would have asked you to do that. It took strength."

"Cut the shit," Rudy said. "It was pure fear. What she did took strength."

"And how is that strength looking?"

"She lost a lot of blood. She's exhausted. She needs rest and fluids . . . and bandages."

"This is the most you've ever said to me, Rudy."

"You're not alone."

Rudy opened the cupboard and grabbed the bandages. He took a bottle of Percocet as well. Sarah stood next to Charlotte and helped sit her up.

"There's water over there," Rudy said. "It's going to hurt like a bitch when she wakes up." He shook the bottle. It rattled closer to empty. Sarah took the water, soaked a towel, and started dabbing away the blood from Charlotte's face. She was careful not to press hard or wipe at the half-frosted, half-soggy mixture around Charlotte's face. It reminded Sarah of a clown, with a red bulbous nose, weird-colored hair, a face painted a ridiculous pale. Sarah never liked clowns. They didn't scare her, but she never understood them. Of all the thoughts she could have had, she didn't know why she thought of a clown. They're meant to be funny, meant to make people laugh but so often make kids cry, too touchy and loud, making crappy balloon animals that look nothing like dolphins.

Charlotte did look more like a clown than Sarah thought, and not just for the horrible paint job Abe had done to her face. The moment Charlotte defeated Abe was a moment they should celebrate; instead Sarah worried, the same as when she had first seen Charlotte's face transformed into something clown-like. Instead of balloon animals, Charlotte gave the settlement a new life, blown up and twisted, big enough for all of them, but they were all still too scared of the clown. The animal Charlotte had made looked nothing like the one they had all asked for.

"Hard," Charlotte squeezed out.

"What?" Sarah asked. Charlotte's eyes stayed closed. Sarah wasn't sure if Charlotte's face looked better or worse with the blood wiped away. The smeared red gave way to black and blue. She resembled a bruised apple. They had plenty of snow to pack against her wounds after they cleared away the streaks of blood.

"Too . . . hard!" Charlotte said. Sarah pressed lighter on Charlotte's cheeks.

"Glad to see you with us," Rudy said. "Can you open your mouth?"

Charlotte widened her jaw a little but struggled.

"That hurt?" Rudy asked.

Charlotte nodded instead of speaking.

"You're going to have to keep your mouth shut as much as possible until your jaw heals. It'll hurt. I'm sure you've noticed. Take these." Rudy put the entire bottle of Percocet in Charlotte's hand and closed her fingers around it. She shook her head.

"It's for the pain," Sarah said. "You need it."

Charlotte shook her head harder and dropped the container.

"No," Charlotte said.

"Don't be stupid," Rudy said.

"She won't do it," Sarah said.

"But—"

"I get it," Sarah told Rudy. "But she said no. Save them for later."

Sarah understood the difference between pain, the layers, the levels, the absences. Sometimes she feared the absence of pain more than the hurt itself. Charlotte must have felt that way, worried that the absence of pain meant she didn't care anymore, even artificially. It wasn't about her body. James was dead. Charlotte carried around the shame, the agony of loss. She had told Sarah when she was locked in the cage. Charlotte didn't want to lose what she thought her last connection to James was, she wouldn't let herself be numbed in case it released her from the only pain that mattered to her, the pain of loss.

Rudy had bandaged Charlotte. He set her left arm in a sling and wrapped her ribs. He tried to reposition her jaw by casing the bandages tight around her head.

"You'll have to forgive yourself eventually," Sarah said. Charlotte looked at her with swollen eyes, filled with the shame Sarah had known was there. "I think this is yours." Sarah placed the stuffed walrus on Charlotte's chest. "Maybe Franklin can help."

Charlotte pressed her head to Sarah's chest and cried. Sarah imagined how the salt in the tears stung worse on Charlotte's wounds than the shame.

UNEARTHED TRUTHS
TIC-TAC

THREE DAYS HAD PASSED SINCE THE ICEDOME. TIC-TAC HAD carried James back to the settlement, with Franklin stuffed into the inner lining of his jacket. He packed James's body with snow until they figured out when the funeral would be before giving the walrus to Sarah. Today Tic-Tac laid the body down in James's old bed. The room hadn't changed. No one had moved in after James left. Mo came to help Tic-Tac with the ritual.

"First time for everything," Mo said.

Tic-Tac said nothing. They stripped the bed of its sheets. They took the bloodstained clothes off James. They dripped warm water over his body and washed away the blood. His smile stayed bright. He looked oddly peaceful in this place of unrest. Tic-Tac and Mo took their time erasing any remnant of a knife mark they could from James's body, except for his smile. That should always stay. They wrapped James in the thin bed sheet.

"We should take him somewhere away from the heat," Mo said. "Otherwise he'll start to smell."

The truth was often the hardest thing to hear because it was the most painful. This truth meant James would sleep forever. Tic-Tac couldn't help him this time. They left James's face unwrapped. They wanted to keep his smile open for everyone to see. *He was dead, but not gone*, Tic-Tac thought.

"It's never easy," Mo said.

"You seem to be fine with it," Tic-Tac said.

"I've never been a people person."

"I wasn't for a long time. Anyone ever tell you why I only played tic-tac-toe for the longest time?"

"I didn't know you did that," Mo said.

"Yeah. I had a stutter. My dad tried to beat it

out of me a few times but it made it worse. By the time my parents were gone, I was too afraid to talk to anyone. I didn't know how they'd react. I was in the hospital with my mom after she 'fell down' the stairs. Some nurse taught me how to play tic-tac-toe. I didn't say much to her but whenever she had a minute she would come by again and we'd play a game or two until she had to check on someone else. When I got to Fornland, it looked like everyone knew how to play. Most kids tried a few times until they got bored with it. But James always played. He never got tired of it—or of me.

"He read a lot back then. He would read out loud on some days and a bunch of us would listen. People thought I loved the stories. I did—I really did, but mainly I heard how words were supposed to sound. I imitated the sounds in my head over and over again. When everyone was asleep I sat in the bathroom and said certain lines over and over again. My favorite was 'when they came closer, they saw

209

that the house was made of bread, and the roof was made of cake and the windows of sparkling sugar.'"

"I had trouble with the 'C' and the 'B.' I loved the idea of an edible house. What kid didn't?"

"I never heard that story before," Mo said.

"You never heard Hansel and Gretel before?"

Mo shrugged. "Different worlds, I guess."

"Doesn't matter. These kids are teased with a candy house and then get captured by a witch. Nothing is ever as sweet as it seems, right?" Tic-Tac and Mo both let out an uneasy laugh. James kept smiling.

"The point is, one night I was staring at myself in the mirror repeating that line. I must have said it twenty or thirty times. On the last time, James spoke up. 'You should try emphasizing the end. Put some force into the *sparkling*.' I didn't know how long he had been standing there, but however long it was, he must have heard me stumble and stammer through the line. He never said anything about it. He took a piss, washed, his hands and said, 'Keep practicing, you'll get there.' He found me standing at the mirror a few times a week, mumbling, and would give me pointers each time. I saved James from drowning once. I don't think he realized what he saved me from."

"He brought me here," Mo said.

"Is that a good thing or a bad thing?" Tic-Tac asked.

"Jury's still out."

Tic-Tac laughed sincerely now. In a few hours they would take the body to the tree line. They would set James on the table and watch the procession of kids kiss their fingers and press them to James's lips one by one. Everyone would say their goodbyes to the kid who didn't know how much he had helped Tic-Tac—how much he had helped them all.

When Tic-Tac and Mo brought James to the tree line the entire settlement was already there. They had been waiting. The sun was out again. The trees dripped with melting ice. The snow was soft.

Tic-Tac's feet sunk a little with each step. They placed James on the table. Gray and Lee sat by his body and pressed their noses to the sheet. They whimpered and pawed at his body, but James stayed still. He won't be coming back this time, Tic-Tac wanted to tell the dogs. They lay down behind the table as if waiting until James sat up to play. Tic-Tac stood by Sarah and Charlotte. Diego and Sand sat near Autry quietly and rested their heads in the snow.

Abe stood distanced from everyone else. Charlotte had said she wanted him there. She wanted Abe to see what he had done. Her jaw had healed over the days but her bruises were as purple as ever. They glistened in the sweat caused by the room's heat. She had taken off the bandage around her head but the ones around her arm continued to support her forearm and ribs.

"I want him to look at himself in everyone else's eyes and see what he's become," she said. "And I want him to know that I'm nothing like him."

Two guards stood by Abe. His face was caked with dried blood and scabs. The rest of the settlement kept their distance. No one wanted to be near him, except Kelsey. She stood close enough for everyone to notice, but not close enough to talk to him. The guards made sure of that.

Charlotte walked up to James's body. She didn't kiss her fingers. She leaned over and kissed his lips. Franklin's head poked out of her coat pocket. His whiskers brushed against James's body when Charlotte leaned in for the kiss. The dogs whimpered. Charlotte stood next to the table as the procession passed by. Each kid kissed their fingers and touched them to James's forehead or cheeks, a quiet and quick farewell.

Shia stepped to the table and looked up at Charlotte. He made to kiss his fingers but instead wrapped his arms tightly around her. Tic-Tac moved to protect her but Shia hadn't attacked.

"I didn't know," Shia said. His voice muffled as he pressed his face to her shoulder. "I didn't know Abe would do that. I thought I could bring it all back together. Then James gave away the food and—"

"It's okay," Charlotte said. "He knew you wanted to help. You didn't know."

How long can a single mistake haunt somebody? Tic-Tac wondered. *How many have already haunted all of us?*

"He never forgave himself for what happened to Marcus. He understood your anger, he told me so. But he trusted you. I trust you too," Charlotte said.

Shia said his goodbye to James. He lingered over the table longer than most people, looking down at the person they all lost, and possibly blaming himself.

Abe was last. His body was tight and he limped when he walked. His face was bandaged around his nose.

"It could've been better," Tic-Tac heard Abe whisper. Abe looked at no one. He held up his hand and showed his missing finger, brushing the phantom finger over his phantom friend. Nothing but ghosts remained. When he walked away, Tic-Tac wanted to force him into the hole that James would soon fill.

"He had saved us all," Tic-Tac told Charlotte. He said it loud enough for Abe to hear. "At one point or another."

"Who the hell is going to save us now?" she asked.

The sun shined on another day. It didn't feel normal yet. Maybe it never would. Whether they all knew it or not, none of them would be here if James hadn't helped. *I wouldn't be here*, Tic-Tac thought. Smoke rose from the volcano. Birds chirped in chaotic rhythms. The days were getting warmer but the settlement felt colder than ever. Charlotte watched over James's body. Mo helped lower James into the ground. Charlotte took Franklin from her pocket and stared at him. The beady eyes looked back, his whiskers motionless.

"You were always around when things changed,"

she said. "Some link to the past. The past is too far gone."

Charlotte had lost any sense of anger. The thoughtful girl Tic-Tac once knew looked closer than ever. She threw Franklin into the hole with James. Mo started to pack the pit with mud and snow. James's body had company in Franklin and both were soon covered. Maybe James had saved Charlotte too, just not in the way they all had thought. The sun drifted over the island and Charlotte stood against the tree line, a regal silhouette forming in the afternoon.